WHEN LOSERS WIN

ANTHONY LABRIOLA

ANAPHORA LITERARY PRESS

DICKINSON, NORTH DAKOTA

Anaphora Literary Press
1053 Koch Street, #210
Dickinson, ND 58601
https://anaphoraliterary.com

Book design by Anna Faktorovich, Ph.D.

Printed in the United States of America, United Kingdom and in Australia on acid-free paper.

Cover Image: Lars Plougmann's "Taylorism" (Wikimedia Commons).

Published in 2026 by Anaphora Literary Press

When Losers Win
Anthony Labriola—1st edition.

Library of Congress Control Number: 2026902857

Library Cataloging Information
Labriola, Anthony, 1950-, author.
   When losers win / Anthony Labriola
   106 p. ; 9 in.
   ISBN 978-1-68114-633-1 (softcover : alk. paper)
   ISBN 978-1-68114-634-8 (hardcover : alk. paper)
   Kindle (e-book)
1. Books—Literature & Fiction—Action & Adventure—War & Military.
2. Books—Literature & Fiction—Genre Fiction—Political.
3. Books—Literature & Fiction—Genre Fiction—Psychological.
PN3311-3503: Literature: Prose fiction
813: American fiction in English

Dedication

To my son, Nic, whose ideas, writings, and images acted as goad, spur, and inspiration for the setting down of this tale.

To Louisa Josephine, Anthony, Michelle, Simon, Nic, Samantha, Lucy, Alice, Christina, Joanna and Masi for their wonderful example during the Pandemic.

To my old friend, George Brasovan, alone in the water.

Part One

1

Shooting Up the Bags

"**A**re *you* Morphy?"

Jack Cade, nicknamed *Lover Boy,*[1] was the guy asking the confrontational question. The answer had to be beautiful, or not at all. He was the edgy, working stiff, the gun-for-hire, and, so far, he was the only ugly loudmouth doing all the talking. A question, but no answer. With an over-the-shoulder glance, the thug he was talking to kept eyeing him. Hard to say what he made of Lover Boy with his big brow bone, or what kind of small-time gangster he took him for. His dirty, blond hair, swept up and piled high on the top of his huge head, was crowned by an untrimmed, Elvis Presley pompadour with long sideburns. In fact, he was known as "the guy with the sideburns." Lover Boy knew his quiff badly needed a cut. As for the other buck, some barber-surgeon had taken a pearl-handled razor to his now hairless head. His shaved skull seemed to delight in being really bald, and took his baldness to heart. Guys without hair likely hate guys with a

---

1   In the beginning, he hated his nickname, until the day came when he grudgingly accepted it as a joke at his expense, and felt worthy of the joke—a moniker that buzzed around him from time to time in the matter of his relationships.

good crop. He wore a form-fitting orange jacket with a glowing yellow X (as a target on his back), heavy-duty work pants with top-loading knee pad pockets and hem guards, and thick-soled shit-kicker boots with reinforced steel-toes.

Lover Boy wore a black bomber jacket, a frayed, black t-shirt, tight-fitting, black jeans, and black steel-toe work boots, imitation shit-kickers. He was asking the question about Morphy, despite a slightly swollen tongue, in order to get what was coming to him. What was coming to Lover Boy was his pay. The limp loop of a mandated mask drooped lazily down over his frost-bitten right ear. He could see the creep he was talking to wasn't wearing a mask. In those days, you had to be careful about masks and mandates. Lover Boy began breathing hard, but still not introducing himself. Maybe, half-hoping that the son-of-a-bitch slouching in front of him wasn't Morphy, not the one he was looking for. Man, he didn't like the look of this buck, and could tell from his sneer that he likely didn't like the dark look on Lover Boy's face either. Mutual disdain and disrespect. Yet sorry to say, Lover Boy was the dude that smelled like dog shit. The other guy didn't. The stink went with the turf. The only work Lover Boy could get at that time was cleaning up after some dog, Morphy's dog, not in the spring thaw, but in the dead of winter. He had left his number on grocery store bulletin boards: "Willing to work, odd jobs." The caller had set up the job with instructions, location, and address for the meet-up upon completion. Lover Boy didn't get the caller's full name, but thought he heard the word *Morphy*, for sure. Of course, he wanted to get paid for the extra effort of finding and shoveling shit buried in snow. So, he went looking for Morphy to get what was owed to him. On that day, as on most days, he really needed the money.

Loaded down, he had a tight grip on two green heavy-duty garbage bags. The turds had once allegedly belonged to Morphy's dog. With no twist ties, Lover Boy had filled the bulging bags to bursting. Too bad he hadn't performed the *poop bag mime*, and just let the crap lie in the snow. He had forgotten to ignore *the stoop and scoop* directive by following it for pay.

"That's how wannabe winners lose," he said.

A guard dog had barked at him in the yard of the compound. Was it Morphy's attack dog? Still, it was at a different location that Lover Boy had cleaned up the mess. A different place, a different dog? Or a different place, but the same animal? Climbing and zigzagging up the backstairs of a four-storey building, Lover Boy had snagged his twin loads on the railing. As he struggled to free the bags, the force of the pull had ripped them apart. After he had gathered and collected the remains of the putrid cargo, torn left and right, slime had oozed and run down the front of his black jeans. Putting the dump bags down, he inadvertently knocked them over, right and left, at the top of the stairs. Pure filth.

This was his current situation. His current situation was similar to previous and long-past situations as well. It seemed that he, Lover Boy, had always been carrying piles of something or other. He looked like a loser, a creep and a freak that deserved to carry dirty bags all his lonely life. It was always somebody else's crap, and rarely, if ever, his own. Not long ago, he came to believe that if he could solve the problem of lifting and carrying such bags, all he'd no doubt gain for his pains would be to get a kick in the ass or a punch in the face. That was the line of thinking that had led him here. Did he even have the right address, let alone the right Morphy? He went where he was told to go.

By the way, should he have taken off his soiled jeans? If he had, he would have to transact business in his underwear. Eventually, or at the first opportunity, he'd have to put them back on, after first using his gloved hands to clean them off with quick, disgusted strokes. When would that be, do you think? He didn't know and couldn't even venture a guess. So, best to keep his black jeans on, he reasoned. He picked up the stinking bags and clutched them tightly. For some crack-brained reason, he was glad he'd kept his shit-smeared jeans on when he dared to ask his anything but beautiful question about Morphy. But, goddammit, was this Morphy the right Morphy, the real Morphy?

"Who's asking?" the right or wrong guy wanted to know.

"You mean, who the hell wants to know, am I right? Is *that* what you're saying?"

"*You* want to know is what I'm saying."

"Yes, I *need* to know."

"Why? Who's this Morphy to *you*? Who are you to *Morphy*?"

"I'm on a *need-to-know* basis these days with every conspirator in this shitty, little town."

"Conspirator?"

"Traitor."

"Psycho?"

"Assassin."

"Snitch?"

"All of the above."

"Well, who are *you*?"

"I'm Jack Cade."

"Never heard of you. What do they call you on the street or in bed?"

"*Lover Boy*. And either you're Morphy, or you're not. Are *you* Morphy?"

All he knew was that some unknown Morphy was supposed to pay him. Was he even at the right place? The way things were going, he'd likely get no pay and a swift kick in the ass for his trouble. How he knew this, he couldn't really say, beyond his usual pessimism. He was convinced that he had earned it, if not deserved it. He was talking about the punishment meted out to flakes like him, doing the dump-ass jobs that losers do, and not getting the cash. In every situation, especially during *those unprecedented days*, as he said to himself, quoting the pundits, he felt he deserved everything he got: nothing, or too little to live on.

"I made it this far," he said. "I shovelled the dogshit and filled the heavy-duty bags. But coming here, I ripped them. Not to worry, I con-solidated what was left of the filth. Then climbed the rest of the stairs, four flights in all. When I found the door opened, I crossed the thresh-old without knocking. As you can see, I passed through, and found you. I made it. If you're Morphy, then pay me. If not, kindly get the hell out of my way. I've got to get the money and fast."

"Or how about getting kicked in the ass, as the crazy case may be, and as it is supposed to be? I could oblige you."

"No, thanks, no obligations, just what is coming to me."

"I'll show you what's coming to you. I can't pretend to know what you're talking about."

"No pretending. I'm owed that much, at least. I don't know what's coming next, but I made an arrangement over the phone."

"Get out of here, before I get riled."

"Wrong room? Wrong guy? Or Morphy *ain't* paying?"

"He always pays."

"But not for the likes of me. Is that what you're trying to get me to understand?"

"I can take care of the filthy likes of you. You're a loser, and losers are born to lose. That's all I'm saying. But you're thick, and you stink."

"Thanks, but, if you're not Morphy, there's nothing for you on this. I got it covered."

"Hey, I *know* one thing, loser."

"That's likely one thing *more* than I know. What do *you* know?"

"How Jack Cade (alias Lover Boy) dies."

"Do your worst, or your best."

The know-it-all guy postured up again. When he withdrew his gun, prepared to shoot, he didn't know what hit him. Two well-positioned bags of dogshit struck him on the left and right sides of his pock-marked face. No sooner was he struck, than he fumbled with his weapon, and dropped it at Lover Boy's feet. The intended victim shuffled and drop-kicked the gun down the stairs.

"I'm Morphy," the guy said, owning his name and identity. "Who did you say hired you? Or was the call a joke, played by some enemy of yours, at your expense, to set you up for clownish disappointment or failure? In that case, you're not only a loser, but a born sucker."

"A sucker?"

Lover Boy could think of one or two jokers that were capable of prank-calling him. One was a player nicknamed Poor Excuse, and another was an idiot he referred to as Tough Luck. Then again, it could also have been an insect-like wheeler-and-dealer he gambled with called Lucky Thing. His name was based on an old joke. He was a joker, and lived to play pranks.

"Let's get this over with," Lover Boy said, dreading that the guy likely had it right about the call and his enemies or oppressors. "I was hired to clean up. I did it, despite soiling myself."

"Drop the bags. Hold still."

Instead of paying him in cash, Morphy punched him in the face, and likely thought he'd broken his nose. But somebody else had already done that.

"Am I supposed to say thanks?" Lover Boy asked, bleeding.

"Don't mention it," Morphy said. "Tough guy, but you can take a punch."

"Why are you giving me the asshole treatment?"

"Take a wild guess."

"Because you think I'm an asshole."

"You act like one, coming here with your story of picking up dog-shit, and wanting to be paid. Still, you get nothing from me, even if one of my people hired you to stoop and scoop. You're too rash in desperately needing cash. You got a dark outlook on life. Now clear out. Be sure to take the bags with you, Lover Boy."

Right before his eyes, what would this Morphy morph into? Lover Boy felt strangely calm after getting punched. Morphy, or the guy calling himself Morphy, shoved him backwards down the first flight of stairs. Burdened as he was, like any falling man, suddenly unemployed once again, with nothing earned for the work he had done, he had no choice, but to twist, turn, trip, and tumble down the rest of the steps. In every sense, he had nothing to show for the job he'd done. When he saw the gun, he asked himself whether he should let it just lie there or pick it up? No, he half-reasoned, he would pick it up and put it in his pocket. This (having a weapon) could be what was supposed to happen *next*. When he struggled to his feet, he oriented his boots in a downward position. Hoisted the bags, not as heavy going down as coming up. Made it down the last flight of stairs to the exit. As he got out of there, he realized that he must have accomplished his *task*, despite not getting the money: he had kept the appointment, despite being disappointed. Even he couldn't call it a real job. What kind of work was that for a man? Though he scoffed at it later on, Lover Boy had done what he thought he was supposed to do. Though he didn't recall, at the time, who had asked him to do it, Morphy in his mockery of him, or some crank-caller calling himself Morphy, had punched him in the face, as *ordained*. Done. He still had a tight hold of the two bags and what was left of the twin loads. With or without malice (it was hard to decide at that moment, and nothing to show for a working man, or the kind of idiot that he took himself to be), he withdrew the gun and shot up the godforsaken bags. In the shoot-out, dog shit shot everywhere. On him, too.

Next.

2

A *Beggin'* Letter

Next, Lover Boy had to deal with the idea of real estate. Yet who was kidding who? Was real estate *the real human estate* for guys like him on the brink of being homeless? An encampment awaited him, or sleeping under a bridge, in a bus shelter, in a bivouac in the Don Valley, or on a park bench in Queen's Park. The idea of owning property was just not really possible anymore, was it?

"The deal and the ideal are not for me," as he liked to say. "Not these days, during the Pandemic with physical distancing, wearing masks, and avoiding social gatherings, and who can own anything, anyway, without real money? Certainly not at the delusional prices they're asking for houses today."

He had rented an apartment in the urban centre. When the Pandemic mandates had made him panic at the global outbreak of Covid-19, he'd moved his family to a rural place out East, a small town, to hide out in. His wife and kids were holed up there. Now, he had two places to pay for, but owned neither one. You see, he didn't want to let the apartment go, not just yet. If he did, he felt that he would never be able to rent one ever again, not for the relatively low rent he was paying in the city.

"You know how it is."

What was the correspondence between heart and home, anyway? It was a false relation, as a result of all the speculation on the housing market.

"Even a dilapidated shit-box, shack or lean-to is going for a sum beyond the asking price."

A place feels like home, or it doesn't. For him, with the fiercely dark mood he was in, identification was tied to identity. Identity gave him personal meaning and some sort of dignity. Losing and lost as he was, it meant he'd lose himself, or was on the verge of doing so, if ever he let go of the two places. Since he couldn't really afford to keep either place, how long could he manage to keep them both? An apartment in the City? A rented house in the Town? About that place, he couldn't even bring himself to say its proper name. Still, he wasn't sure of his relationship with either location.

"Touch and go, incomplete, resentful, shameful at best."

He always blamed himself for his sense of loss and corresponding sense of shame.

"What if I want to go back?" he kept saying. "Everything's so uncertain. How can I foretell what is supposed to happen next? Who knows why these things happen to me, and how things will turn out?"

The apartment in the city gave him a kind of urban identity. He had studied there. Married there. Had had children there. The apartment was their first family home. His identification with it had something to do with what he believed he had to do *next*. What? Decide? Pay for both? Default? What the hell was he going to do next? Next, he had to beg, despite his fast-growing identity crisis. He had to write a begging letter, and make copies, begging for cash, begging for a handout. Wasn't he worthy of getting help? Whom could he turn to? He really thought that money was a way out of his present predicament. On the other hand, the harder he worked for it, the less he seemed to have.

Lover Boy reasoned (perhaps badly) that, although making decisions had paralysed him during Lockdown, money (real money) would get him moving again. Him, and all the girls in his world. But those were the poor days. His days were poor. Yes, his impoverished days were rich in poverty. He didn't earn his days or its wages. Instead, he bought them on credit as they carried the weight of his mortgaged time with high interest rates. Financial advisers talked about wealth management, but he had to manage *desperate times*, especially when the poor days couldn't be avoided.

He walked down to the creek that his wife and kids called the Babbling Brook, ditched the shot-up bags, looking a little like big, deflated balloons, sat on the bank, and wrote his notorious *beggin'* letter, as he called it, *beggin'* for time, *beggin'* for mercy and *beggin'* for money, with a tiny pencil in a small notepad that Lover Boy kept in his back pocket. How do you ask somebody for money? Come to think of it, he was always *beggin'*: *beggin'* for love or *beggin'* for mercy and *beggin'* for money. When he was a kid, he'd beg for something he couldn't have. Later, he would beg for a kiss, or a feel, or a peek. He begged others, and they begged him not to. When he got old, if he made it to old age, he'd still be *beggin'*, even for his life, or especially. *Beggin'* at his own door: the beggared description of rain falling in the alley was enough. Of all the hideouts, this one was hidden on the slippery slope of the *beggin'* years. With the prickly ache in his twisted fingers, he wanted to secure the frayed rope, just before jumping over the naked puddles outside his own door to hide himself, lift out of the mud and float above the trees, a grey body hanging from a leafy bough. "*Jump, jump,*" the hidden voices rose up from the past, ghosting his cries, and the moment arrived when all he had was everything he ever owed. And his debt was resentment, not gratitude, a beggar *beggin'* at his own door for something he didn't own. Now, he had his *beggin'* letter.[2]

---

2   The letter went something like this:

"Forgive me (or don't, as you see fit) for writing to you after so many silent years. Absence during the Pandemic has put a chokehold on the heart. Is it fonder or less fond? As you might have guessed, I need your help. Help me. I'm beggin' you, even as it sticks in my throat to say so. I'm reaching out to you wherever you are. Do I really need your help? That has yet to be determined. I suppose I need to convince you. I recall what you said that last time that I was bleeding all over you: 'Where are your relatives?' I said: 'I don't know: same place, I suppose. Nowhere to be found.' So, I'm begging you for help, just in case it's your help that I really need. Beggin'? Can you hear my voice in this? Do I have to get on my hands and knees? I'll leave the amount up to you. It's never enough, right?

"This is a beggin' letter. I'm crawling, crawling back to you. Let me say it right off so that you can decide what to do with it before you read any more of what I have to say. Go ahead. Put it in the trash. Recycle it. Burn it if the thought of me beggin' for your help disappoints you, angers you, riles you. I'm hurt, but who hurt me? Right? Is it any easier on you to say that I hurt myself? In your outrage, watch this letter burn to ashes. Flush them down the toilet. It's just waste. And as such, doesn't deserve your consideration, kind or unkind, as the case may be.

Getting to the point is what I'm trying to do, despite the circling round and round the money issue. I've already begged at my own door. Nothing doing. I turned myself away. I said, 'Get lost: you're undeserving of pity and alms, a handout, or a leg up. Get out of here.'

Have I tried a paper coffee cup held out to passersby, for instance, to see what coins I can get? Have I sat on a milkcrate, panhandling? Have I used a slogan or a chant to draw attention to my plight? Plight? I mean, the fix I was/am in? Guess.

"No, don't waste your breath guessing, or even thinking about it. I'll tell you later, if it comes up again. Why did I not succeed? Because. Why did I fail? For the same reason. Was I simply not lucky? Not lucky enough? Was I fortune's fool? Or just a fool. Did I give everything away? Grasshopper, rather than ant. 'Why do you hoard?' 'Why do you waste?' That hellish battle even in hell. Does it have anything

Wouldn't you know it? He didn't have any stamps to put on the envelope. Anyway, Lover Boy didn't have an envelope to mail his *beggin'* letter. He'd have to hand-deliver it, or a copy of it, if he could only remember the address(es), and if he could get there. Would anybody let him in? He thought of *beggin'* Florinda, an old girlfriend of his that he'd once cheated on. If she refused to see him, he'd try the philanthropic Dr. Sparrow, his on-again, off-again therapist and tormentor. What about *beggin'* Tad Spinski, his filthy-rich but spiteful brother-in-law, a real adversary? And Lover Boy was prepared to take money even from his own mother, if it ever came to that, and if she could bear the sight of him after all the trouble that he had caused her. Then he would have to wait for the *verdict*: would anybody help him? Help or no help, with his hand palm-upwards, he had the *beggin'* letter: a grocery list of wants and needs, an absurd litany of complaints, grievances, justifications and absurd excuses for the folly of his poverty. Everybody seemed to be making a killing, but him. He was killing himself for little or nothing, or the whole thing was a put-on. *Next.*

---

to do with it? 'Why did I flop? Why did you succeed?' Feed me, feed me. Why do you save? Need or greed? So, you won't have to beg? Why do you spend? So, you will have to beg. What does the almsgiver know that the beggar doesn't? What good can you do with money? What good can you do without it? No money. No mercy. What has happened to me? What has befallen your past acquaintance? I have nowhere to turn, and no one to turn to. Why must you be acquainted with my grief? Why do you have contempt for me, enough to watch me falter, fail and fall? Do you want to miss out on this opportunity to show compassion? All right, it's my fault, my fault entirely. Am I looking for a handout or a loan? Well, I'm up to my neck in debt. Yes, I'm in the shit. Take it from there. So, help me, for mercy's sake. Or just throw this letter away. In an ironic sense, losers win by not wanting to play. Yours, Jack Cade."

3

Door of Her Refusal

Next, he had to deal with his wife—talk about a collector of grievances—a woman he'd nicknamed Priscilla, in honour of the King's one-and-only bride. Lover Boy's Priscilla had little or nothing in common with Priscilla Presley, but had let him call her whatever he wanted to, even though she could never quite get him to say her real name, *Mariya*. He also had to contend with another woman, a part-time lover named Zouzou Laylah, that he liked to call "The Lips." He could never figure out if that was her real name or not, or just a stage name, a pseudonym, or even if the name was supposed to be spelled Zouzou, or Zou-Zou. His relationships with these two women were unstable, indefinable, on-again off-again, to say the least, much like the places where he had been destined to live from time to time.

When he met up with Priscilla, would she pull a *Morphy*? Would she smack him or kick me where it counts, and then kick him out? Would she offer to blow him away for the way he'd been hurting her? He realized that, despite her derision, she knew he was *love-tormented*. Yet he preferred to say that he was *sex-starved*. He liked to say that the *woman* he wanted was the kind of beauty that had to be seen to be believed. That was the truth he carried in the muscle of his heart and the one in his groin. He guessed that both women knew it only too well.

He and Priscilla had once been locked together in a crowded apartment. The bond of blood between them flowed through their two kids, Ana and Lina. But they didn't live together for long without bumps and interruptions, threats and allegations, including intervals of separation. They lived apart from time to time and with other people, too.

For Priscilla, Lover Boy appeared at times to be a freak, a player, and a hound. Man, he acted like a sweet cheat. Also, her adversary. She knew that she had to be on her guard against her husband's sneak attacks. He was always up for betrayal, parading as freedom and self-expression. His so-called rebellion could easily undermine the shaky order of their vicious marital arrangement. Though he called it *virtuous*, Priscilla referred to it as *malicious*. Which was it? Maybe, it was both. He said that though he had no real history or any place in it, he liked to think of himself as *Jack Cade*, the rebel in Shakespeare. *That* Cade's rebellious speeches spoke of social grievances and anti-authoritarian feelings to support his rebellion. What was *this* Jack (Lover Boy) Cade's rebellion in aid of?

"The bandit is always waiting to jump you," Priscilla said to anyone who would listen to her lamentations, even the kids. "Or Lover Boy enjoys horning in on the action. That is, if he isn't pleasuring himself."

For his part, as a kind of insanity defense, he said, in light of the evidence, "Everything I've ever done, I've done for women, including the abovementioned *pleasuring*."

Was it another way of saying that how he acted towards them was really and entirely for himself, and against them? Priscilla thought so, and had once said so. Lover Boy's disappointed bride, that is, his *faithless love*, or his *despised love*, as he said of her, with or without justification, was *sweet Priscilla*, as he used to call her. She had come to realize that she wasn't enough for him. She certainly would have been enough for any other guy, like No Chance, and even Tough Luck.

Yet *longing* was the word Lover Boy associated most with his other love, Zouzou, known as *The Lips*. He had read somewhere that her name meant "Come on. Let's go." He liked that. The word *impossible* was also a part of his liking for these two women. Yes, he had to have them *both*. He wanted sex badly. *Badly*. That was correct: he wanted to make it with somebody else's wife again and again, but still cling to, and smother, his own. Was he suffocating them both? He thought they hated him deep down, each in the pit of her own guts, in her own particular way, and for her own special reasons. The women knew that he didn't stand a chance, if ever he had to decide between them. Lover Boy felt that he wasn't lucky in many things, including money, and true love was certainly one thing he had no luck with, if his life were seen as a card game. How do you choose when it's all based on chance?

"Everybody wants to straighten me out," he said. "Truth is, like every goof, I hate to be left out, or cut off."

Lover Boy just went on and on about his desire, his dignity and sense of self when he wasn't wanted. Refusal and rejection were poisons to him. He didn't know which woman to choose, but he wanted them to choose him, and only him. In times of loneliness, he choked and gagged on being alone.

"Bullshit," one of the women had said, scoffing, but he couldn't remember which one. "You always look for ways to be by yourself."

It had started with emotional intimacy and had ended with just plain going to it, as they used to say in those sex-filled days and nights of the world in the Time of Disease for deniers and believers alike. But not everybody wanted *tenderness*.

The others thought (or he had led them all to believe) that the ass-hole (Lover Boy) had reformed, and that he had changed to the point of tenderness. Had he finally learned how to decide? Were they blind? Had he really lost his edge, his viciousness? Was that what he was really working on as a personal project? What kind of work was that? Had he opted for virtuous attachments, moving from violence to coopera-tion? Both *forces* (his conception) had once jumped him in a creek-side ambush. They had tied his thick wrists and ankles with long ropes and had dragged his captured, shocked body down the slope under the bridge only to hurl him into the creek. One of them had pulled on the one side, and the other along the farther bank, and had dragged his drowning body through the water. He could either sink or plead his case and state that he'd been baptized (or something) by women to escape drowning. He could make a decision and choose between them before they let him go under. But he refused to be rescued. He couldn't.

Simply because he had tried and failed, didn't mean that anybody else had to believe him. Whose fantasy was this, anyway? What dark purpose did it serve? It never happened, but he wished it had as in a dream to intensify his feelings about the women. After pretending to, with crazy allegations, accusations, rumours, ambiguities, lies and con-tradictions, he felt he had to set the record straight in his own way and on his own terms. And maybe, he'd be able to set the world straight, too, a world that was now dying in the millions from a deadly Virus. For a creep and a loser, his tale should have been called *I Would Have Won*. That was right: a game that he would have won, if only he could have won it without cheating. He convinced himself in a contradictory way that he could win any game that he didn't really want to play.[3] That was the perversity of a twisted tale that he was repeatedly telling himself.

"You win when you don't want to win," he said. "That's how losers win: no losing that way. So, too, you can't win, if you don't play."

3   *Jokers Wild* by Nic Labriola.

Setting others straight by playing a game or not, cracking jokes about winning or losing, wired to reduce everything to farce was something he'd been doing ever since he was a kid in elementary school. Lover Boy had to beat the shit out of everybody when he tried to protect Priscilla from other boys, especially a kid nicknamed No Chance. They had known each other a long time. On the school yard, Lover Boy had pulled out the tiniest jackknife his intended victim had ever seen when he'd threatened to stab No Chance, aged 7 or 8, with it.

"I tried to jab him in the face," Lover Boy said. "Another time, I tried to choke him. But he put a scissor-lock on me, clamping his legs around my ribs. Even while I was losing air, he soon let me up and told me to make snowballs for him. He threw them into my face, while I just stood there taking it. Then when I was sixteen, there was the beating somebody laid on me in Montreal for being there with his girl, Florinda. (I'll be sure to look her up again.) Still, I always got and get everything wrong. That's when I realized that I always would."

Always?

"In the first place," he said, "I got everything wrong about girls, especially my belief that a dude had to have sex with 10,000 chicks, or he wasn't a real dude. But is a woman that I make love to 10,000 times good enough for me? Isn't it better that way? Do I like slickness in the matter of sex? Or depth?"

His real problem was money, not sex. Getting it. Holding on to it. Paying for two places and two women at the same time: that was the trouble. Things always came in twos for him. They doubled and double-downed on him until they double-crossed him altogether.

"Always had to take care of myself with little or no money in the bank," he said. "I worked all the time. But wasted it all. I had to be told off."

"Big spender has to be told," Priscilla said.

She told him.

"When the time comes, I'll be sure to show him," Zouzou said. "One of us will lose him. One of us will win him."

"But I can't lose, if I don't want to play," he said. "I just can't keep beating myself at my own game."

"Right, he has to be told," one of the two women said.

"Deluded bastard has to be shown," the other one said. "Too bad I love him."

"Too bad for me, too."

He had to win at his own losing game. Couldn't they see that? Then why was he always playing other people's foolish games, a poor player, or some kind of bad jester? He couldn't solve that riddle either.

4

A Tale of Two Women

He set off on foot to see *what-was-her-name*? Priscilla, his wife. Not the other one?

"No, not *what's-her-name*? The one with The Lips."

The other woman had a name, as mentioned, but he preferred not to use it, if he could avoid it. She wasn't his wife, but another man's woman, as she liked to say, despite the folks that it pissed off. The guy was the guy that Lover Boy had nicknamed No Chance back in school, now grown-up, a magnificent cuckold, and the one that was perpetually cheated on. Though Lover Boy had known him since they were kids, he never really knew where he was now, or what he was up to. Lover Boy was in no position to tell him.

His decision, if he could call it that, not to see the woman with perfect lips right off or straightaway drove him crazy. At least, the memory of her lips did. He wasn't sure that he had made the right choice to stop by and see Priscilla first, but he needed an envelope and stamps. Anyway, he had to walk along the King's Highway 2 to get there. Still, he had to see his wife first, deal with the begging letter, and then move on to Zouzou.

"Maybe, I should have gone to see her first," he said.

Less fraught, but farther away.

"Less messy," he said, "and less noisy, but it's the natural order of things for someone like me."

Priscilla lived in the rented house in a small town that the family had gone to in order to escape the Virus; and the other one lived in the apartment that Lover Boy had rented in the city. Sometimes, he wanted to switch it up, but hesitated at the last moment, and couldn't decide which one to keep and which one to get rid of.

"Shouldn't have set them up in different places," he said. "Couldn't figure it out, though. Needed time to, job or no job. So, that's what I had to do."

He was going to ask Priscilla for an envelope to mail his begging letter. A stamp, too. She would give him what he wanted or she wouldn't.
All the houses on the street looked the same. He recognized the place
by the stroller on the snow-covered lawn, the toys on the front steps,
and a long-handled shovel he'd put there for winter. It was the same
shovel that Lover Boy had used to scoop and load the dog shit into the
bags. Should he knock? Was the door locked? Probably. He searched
for the key. Wrong one. That was the apartment key. When he found
the one for the house, he used it. Went in. Where was Priscilla? Where
was the dog? Their dog, not Morphy's. Where was everybody: wife,
dog, kids?

"Should I just leave well enough alone? Should I leave, and let them
alone, and let them be?"

Priscilla had heard him coming in. She let him wander around for a
while and then stepped out to greet her husband. It began right away:
the talking. That is, when she decided to talk to him. It didn't go well.
They picked up where they had left off: old arguments, old questions
and answers, accusations and evasions. She had all the answers. He had
all the evasions. She had her own suspicions, and worried about what
he was up to, and what he was going to do next. He didn't have a single
answer that satisfied her, as always. When he asked for an envelope, she
told him to get it himself.

"You know where they are, if there are any left," she said. "Don't
wake the baby. I just put her down."

Lover Boy ranged around the house. It looked familiar and yet un-
familiar to him at the same time. Either it was his rented house or
it wasn't. Each room had lost more and more traces of him. He was
disappearing. Never mind the envelope. He wouldn't send a letter, but
hand-deliver his request for help. He had to get out of there fast. He
stood face-to-face with Priscilla. Moved in for a kiss. She let him kiss
her, sort of. She had her mouth closed. He kissed her teeth. When he
left, he thought he heard her say: "When are we going to stop this
charade?" She could say things like that, and she had said them before,
because she knew secret things about him that no one else knew, or
pretended not to know. For one, that he'd had a heart attack. He wore
the scar to prove it. As it turned out, Zouzou said she liked scars when
she touched his chest, and even enjoyed kissing it, but never asked him
what it was from, a knife attack of one kind or another.

With Priscilla, at that moment, it was bad enough not to see the baby and not to wait for the other child to come back from school, but worse was that while he was wandering around the house, he wasn't thinking of them at all, not even the dog. He was thinking of the other woman, the one with the perfect lips that he longed for so much. Yes, he was there with Priscilla, but at the same time, he was thinking about the other one, and wishing she were there, and that he was over there with her at the apartment in the city, and not in this rented house in the small town that he had been forced to move to so as to escape the Pandemic, more of a threat in the Big City. At that time, he had come to believe that, since there were fewer citizens in a smaller town, it must mean there was less risk of contracting Covid-19.

The thing about the other woman was that she was Priscilla's look-alike, a dead ringer. They could have been sisters, twins, spitting images, at least. Though Zouzou was a native of B.C. (Gabriola Island) and Priscilla was born and raised in P.E.I., they should not have resembled each other, but did. Did one islander look like another as far apart as east to west and coast to coast. Lover Boy loved both extremes.

Strange thing was that Lover Boy hadn't noticed the resemblance at first. Neither had he realized what the strange fascination was for women that mirrored each other. The other woman's lips, yes, and there were the kisses, but it seemed the curve of her mouth was slightly different from that of Priscilla's, and that made a world of difference, made all the difference in the world, and the matter of carrying on with two women who looked so much alike, only laterally inverted, what did it really matter? Who was he to want the one and the other at the same time? It was like a town he had to live in and a city he wanted to live in at the same time. He kept wanting the one that was left behind since he couldn't reside in both places at once. What was revealed in his mind that had for a time eluded his eyes was how identical the women and the circumstances were.

"My own peculiar or particular tale of two cities," he said in a joking tone, "and the hilariously sad story of two women who shouldn't resemble each other, almost as tears do, but do look amazingly alike. How do you deal with something as crazy as that?"

5

Florinda

Lover Boy's deal was that in the face of time passing (it seemed like day for night, and night for day, but it was likely and simply a trick of time), he kept saying over and over again:

"Is this what I was thinking about: of Florinda, a woman I had known before I met Zouzou and the one I cheated on even as I headed towards her and back and forth to and from Priscilla?"

He headed towards her now, ready to beg, if he had to, and as he wanted to, for financial help. But could he touch her for money? And, after how mean he had been to her in the past, would she ever let him touch her?

"You came, Lover Boy," Florinda said, opening the door to him. "It has been how long, too long? Look at you. Were you in a car crash?"

"I fell down a flight of stairs," he said. "I was in a one-sided fight. I apparently lost the last match against my own shadow. My opponent clobbered me. Thanks for seeing me, Florinda."

"Sit down. Do sit down, old friend. Take it easy. Can I get you anything? Coffee? Bandages? Painkillers?"

He sat down, as if his sagging body were saying, achingly:

"Help me. Let me come to a resting position to avoid perpetual motion."

She sat close to him, too close, as she always did in the past.

"Do you really want to be fighting?" she asked, agonizingly thinking how terrible he looked, and how wounded and defeated he was.

"Sometimes, I can't help it," he said, "losing, I mean. But I don't want to win, I guess. That gives me the illusion of winning somehow in an ironic and twisted sense."

"If we only knew what was good for us," Florinda said, "but sometimes, we can't win, or can't lose. We're just sad, disappointed. Isn't that funny?"

"Always been difficult to distinguish between the two," he said. "The sadder it is, the funnier it seems. Well, for winners, like the shadows we box, and losers, anyway, like me, it has to be ironic, you see, because I'm not given to luck. I'll have to give it more thought, if I can make it. So, what are you doing these days, Florinda?"

"Just working on my projects, you know, flowers and crafts, as you know."

"I remember. Everything natural."

"This is how we should all live, I think," she said, "in nature."

"Just the way flowers do?" he said, remembering that she had been named for the Roman goddess of flowers.

"Exactly," Florinda said. "They've been around since the beginning. I wish I were a flower. You need taking care of, Lover Boy, just like a wilted flower," she added in a sudden, but natural flush.

"I'm wilted for sure," he said.

He wanted nothing better than to be tended to, like a flower, with light and water, and away from the pain of love and work. He had once loved her dearly, deeply, inevitably, wounded as he was even then, switching the order of things, or in an attempt to re-establish some kind of natural order.

What did his past love for her and her "acceptance of nature" have to do with his present *need*? Did she have money, the kind of money to give or lend to someone that had betrayed her so long ago? How could he even bring himself to the point of asking her? He was on the verge of either asking or leaving.

"We were good together back in the day," Florinda said.

"It was good."

How could he ask her now?

"We were good for each other," Florinda said, as if speaking in shades of blue irises. "You, me: it was a sort of complete situation, if you get my drift or gist, or just remember."

"I get the drift, and I remember," he said.

"If you recall, there was tenderness between us until the hurt."

"I do."

"Lover Boy, Lover Boy, you left me for her," Florinda said in hushed tones, "your childhood sweetheart, Priscilla. Or, you went back to her would be more accurate, more vengeful. You broke my heart, *but*."

"It was a bloody incident that time," he said, "the worst kind, I admit."

Guilt, shame, even revenge, how could he make up for what he had done to her, as if he couldn't help it, and as if it had to happen: to hurt someone in order to be with someone else? Did it have to be that way?

"Well, here we are," Florinda said. "What brings you here, Lover Boy, really?"

"It's a vague desire to fix things, to get things right."

"Between us?"

"No, not necessarily between *us*. It occurs to me that I shouldn't have come."

"There is in you, Lover Boy, a vagueness, and always has been," Florinda said, "that can influence you in a positive or negative way, and both at the same time. You step into misery, instead of staying clear of it."

"I'm vague," he said, "and can't decide things these days. Never could. It's miserable. No certainty, for sure."

"But it can be of use," she said, "especially when things begin, but not in matters of love."

He wasn't sure how to take it: her view of things, especially in the matter of love. What had happened to make him hate it all? To go on with, one of them had to choose to say something.

"Choose me, Lover Boy," Florinda said, leaning close to him, too close.

"Right," he said, remembering, and recalling, too, that he could hurt her badly.

"Here," she said, giving him a plucked flower.

What was the link between this flowering moment and the begging scheme he was working on? He figured that moving towards Florinda had something essential and something ultimate to do with it, but couldn't think of just what that was, not right now, because, right now, *right now*, his thoughts were drifting in a wide-open sky of pretend-love and near self-deception, and his judgement, such as it was, was off. It hurt when she touched him. He closed his eyes and let himself drift for a while, in the garden of her room, and soon fell into a half-sleep, so terribly exhausted, the edge of gloom, and so much in pain.

Why was he there? He must have looked terrible, exhausted, beaten. She searched through his pockets and found his begging letter, crumpled. He let her. She read it as he rested, or came to rest. Then replaced it. *Money*. It was about money. When he finally opened his eyes and looked at her, he said:

"You were always so mischievous, facetious, Florinda, as the bouquets swirled above your head, like something out of Chagall."

"No, I'm on your side, Lover Boy, not laughing up my sleeve, and not just tending my own garden, but I don't have much money to give you or lend you. I gave you myself, but it wasn't enough. It cost me dearly."

"I'm *beggin'*," he said, tasting the rust on his tongue in saying the word.

"I know, but you're not a real beggar," Florinda said. "You're only pretending. You don't know how to fall on your knees. You don't know how to beg. Could you beg in the street, Lover Boy, a panhandler?"

"We'll see."

"Can you say to somebody (without it sticking in your throat): 'I'm begging you?'"

"I'm begging you."

"Begging?"

"*Beggin'.*"

"For what?"

He said it, reluctantly, as it stuck in his throat: "*Beggin'* for money. *Beggin'* for time. *Beggin'* for work. *Beggin'* for love and mercy."

"Lover Boy, you can't even say it right. It's not convincing."

Inauthentic, a fake, phoney, a wannabe, a fraud, an imposter: what she really thought of him, no doubt trying to get back at Lover Boy, avenging herself for his past cruelty. Spite, resentment. Scorned as she had been, she was now vengeful. What was he supposed to do… beg for forgiveness for the horror of his history?

"Why don't you work with me in the garden?"

"What would you pay me?"

"What I can skim off the top of my wages."

"Can I raise a family on working with flowers?"

"A family?"

"A family, and two places, bills, and living expenses. Is it enough?"

"Is it ever? I wasn't enough for you. Why weren't we good enough for each other?"

When he didn't say anything, she stepped out, and when she came back, she fanned a few $20 bills, like a small bouquet, that she held out for him to take. He stood up.

"Sorry," he said, but refused to take the cash, because this time enough was still not enough.

"Don't be a choosy beggar, Lover Boy, in love or money."

"It was wrong of me to come here. Wrong choice, even for a *bad* beggar."

"It was great to see you," Florinda said, still holding onto her little offering.

"Thanks," he said, making a slapstick exit by placing one of Florinda's flowers with a broken stem between tightly clenched teeth, realizing how funny his unhappiness was, and he left, clownishly hurt and comically hurting.

6

40, 000 Brothers

He found himself drifting in the direction of his spiteful brother-in-law, Tad Spinski. Actually, he was aiming right for Tad to target him for a handout. They had fought over the years, and once or twice, had even come to blows over their irreconcilable differences, and still couldn't stand each other. The only thing they had in common was Priscilla. Of course, Tad called her *Mariya*. Her brother was a successful entrepreneur and business executive. Lover Boy never really knew what his lunatic brother-in-law, as he called him, bought and sold or even dealt in. Spinski always said that he was luckier than the rest, luckier than this loser, for sure. For Spinski, having a Business Plan was some kind of universal truth. Money was money, and money was the meaning of the universe. Money was his. He knew how to make it, and better, how to keep it. Could Lover Boy touch him for any of it? That was yet to be seen. He realized that he couldn't hesitate or quaver in his resolve to get cash, no work, no pay, no matter how disrespectful Spinski was towards him.

"If this has got something to do with my sister, I might have to bend a bit, but not for your sake, Cade. Just remember that. Are you afraid of something?"

"I'm not sure if *afraid* is the right word for it when I'm out to get something from you, something I know you don't like to part with. But I don't want to end up cowering in a corner from fright, I don't know, and I'm not sure if I'm unable to get out of my inert situation, even when I think I'm finished."

"So, you got into trouble again, the same nasty business once more, the *poverty* you have plunged your family into, am I right?"

"I'm into it to save them, Tad. And you're a part of the story, or the fiction that I'm believing, or trying to, if you choose to be."

"And what have I to do with any of this?"

"Not sure, but hoping you could tell me, *or* help me with the search for the truth of making money."

"And here you are looking for God knows what exactly, nothing beyond extortion, am I right? Or just on your knees begging, because you're a perpetual beggar in the disguise of a wounded man."

"On my knees? Do I look it?"

"You're bent down, soon kneeling, then crawling. I'm looking for signs that you're not here to beg."

"Need?"

"You make me laugh. Need?"

"Want? I'm looking for evidence of compassion."

"Giving a shit as a rich man? Feelings?"

"Giving a shit, yes. You're right there, Tad. Do you care?"

"About what, Cade? You start something, but soon give up before it pays any dividends. You're a quitter, like those that kill themselves. Only yours is a monetary suicide. You also leave things and people behind. You desert them. You're a deserter, aren't you? Did you turn your back on the military? Didn't you desert the armed forces? Some kind of traitor to this country?"

"I served part-time with the Regular Forces."

"Your deployment wasn't exactly a success, was it? Weren't you up on charges?"

"Look, I did what I was told. When it was over, I got out. It wasn't a career path for me, Tad. I was no traitor and I didn't desert."

"Permanently AWHOL."

"I didn't exactly love it."

"Then do something you love. Don't abandon it."

"Thanks for caring,"

"I care and I don't care: it's a strategy. I'm a strategist. That's what I do. That's who I am."

"And what are the rest of us?"

"Stupid, especially about work and money. And for you, Cade, don't tell me it's your wife, my sister, Mariya. Do you love her, or even care about her the way I do?"

"It seems to me that the care of 40, 000 brothers like you, Tad, won't ever equal to how I feel about her."

"40, 000 brothers? What are you saying?"

"I think I'm quoting Hamlet, if I remember."

"You're no Hamlet. You're just the jester. Alas, poor Lover Boy, as they call you, nobody knows you as well as I do. Do you ever get love or money right?"

"Maybe, maybe not. We'll see how it turns out."

They continued the negotiations, or whatever this exchange was be-yond a pissing match, in the same vein as any losing game. You had to piss with the big dogs. According to Spinski, Lover Boy would sabotage herself. Either way, it wasn't fair. He didn't deserve to lose, and Spinski didn't deserve to win all the time. But he did, and the fact that he did, made Spinski appear invincible. They would destroy what they had made, them, those eternal, Lover-Boy-like losers and failures. Spinski would always win. He did eventually get around to Lover Boy being in a fog, and that his head was in the clouds, and so on. And Lover Boy did come back with the notion of brain fog, and other weather condi-tions of the mind. His words meant little or nothing to his brother-in-law, let alone Lover Boy's analogies and insights.

"Hope you don't lose your way, or your head, while begging. Or is the truth about making money? You get *nothing* from me. For you, money is never enough. It never lasts long enough to make a difference. I already gave my sister funds to get you out of trouble before."

Since Spinski gave him nothing, Lover Boy was forced to move on, with nothing. He moved on with *squat*, because he had no ironic op-tion, no alternative, or even a comedic comeback, and didn't deserve to stay. The only thing he could do was to crack himself up. The laughable truth was that even humour failed him now. No option. No mockery, but self-mockery. He was just making faces at his failure. Spinski was the better marksman, sharpshooter where words were concerned. Lov-er Boy couldn't think of a sure-fire joke or pun or punchline (at anyone else's expense) to make himself laugh, let alone a man as humourlessly rich and expensively grim as Tad Spinski.

7

No Begging or Solicitation

"**N**o beggars or solicitors," Dr. Sparrow was saying to him when he greeted Lover Boy at the door of his historical place downtown with an old-fashioned porch wrapped around it and a vast yard sprawling out back, and let him in. It could have been the door of his refusal, as it had been in the distant past, but today it wasn't refusal but acceptance.

Lover Boy listened and talked, talked and listened, like a patient. Dr. Sparrow had counselled him about 10 years ago and even after when Lover Boy felt he just couldn't go on. Though the doctor was big on meaning, Lover Boy seldom, if ever, knew what he meant.

"Begging and soliciting cause pain," he said. "I know that much. Things fall apart."

"There are signs *everywhere* of collapse."

If there were signs to interpret, where were they? If he couldn't read them, were they beyond figuring, or just for a chosen few, and written in an indecipherable code to mystify guys like Lover Boy?

"I use the ideas of Dr. Viktor Frankl, and his search for meaning, paradoxical intention, and trying to help us to overcome fear by laughing at ourselves, and his focus on the reality of love. Is it about pleasure? Is it about power? Is it about meaning? Is it about love?"

"Reality checks?"

"Remember, you first came here asking for help with your need to fall in love, or at least, to ask everyone you met in those days to have sex with you."

"Florinda?"

"She was a special case. Her treatment involved helping others, and, of course, her disorder, which she told me you knew about with her flower fixation. She suspected you'd fallen in love with her. You were hopelessly in love with Florinda, weren't you?"

"I suppose so, if a declaration of love is in order."

"But how does anyone know if it's real love?"

"I don't."

"Making a decision is everything. You choose whatever gives meaning to your life, and you *will* it to happen or take place, according to Dr. Frankl?"

"Will it?"

"You have the free will to choose."

"It isn't always free. There's a cost. It's like choosing one form of sadness over another. It's all sad."

"But you need a pure heart and clean conscience to choose. What about your wife?"

"What about her?"

"What about your feelings for her?"

"Complicated, based on our teenage song-of-songs, especially when you also love someone else, or think you do, or just want to. Have you ever treated her?"

"I'll tell you: I'm trying to deal with the way she bleeds for you, and the guilt and shame of loss she carries in the pit of her gut, *but*."

"But?"

"But that's the least of her troubles."

"The least? What's the most?"

"Her biggest problem is that she sees the connection between *who* we are and *where* we live. Identification with a place and the sense of personal identity we derive from it. You once loved Mariya so much being away from her that you dreamed up a life whereby you could rename her, subtract her on a daily basis, take a lover, chip away at her esteem and dignity, and still call it love, a love that had to be paid for, not by sacrifice, but by money. That is, a life split in two. Not only polyamory, but a tale of two cities and two women. In your case, all will be revealed. Nothing will be lost once you decide between places to live and people to care for. Everything will be reclaimed, regained. The only things lost will be lies. It's part of the healing process for Mariya, and you, too. And you haven't lost time or much else with this need of yours to be punished, to atone for something, and beg for money."

"I've lost my cash."

"No, not even that."

"Where is it then?"

"You regret losing. But you would have regretted winning. If you beg, you'll regret it.[4] If you don't beg, you will regret it. Why not be as poor as you can be, and stop trying to avoid poverty, and just laugh at it? Laugh at the situation. Laugh at yourself. I hope I've provided you with a way of seeing things. Well, anyway, you're a collector of grievances. I suppose you'll continue to grieve."

"How funny is that, especially for a sick man?"

"Well, good, despite your sneers, and since you're not an invalid, and since I've warned you before about invalidism, be careful, and take special care of yourself and your family. Now, I suggest you have a little chat with the one person that you have been avoiding in your round of begging."

"My mother, and all her maternal absurdities?"

"Yes, but be careful in dealing with your mother. Sorry I'm unable to give you any cash, owing to the fact that I don't believe in handouts for my patients, past or present, and since I don't run a charitable organization, I have different notions of mercy and compassion."

Dr. Sparrow had a funny way of showing how different his notions were from Lover Boy's.

"I showed you in," he said, grimacing, "now you show yourself out."

Acceptance, and then refusal: it was through the same door in and out. At that, knowing he was offering Lover Boy nothing beyond adapting to his own suffering, and getting on with it, for his disappearing act, he did a weak and awkward mock-shuffle, gave a little nervous laugh, and two-stepped his way out, though he'd never learned to dance.

"Doctor, I was left *beggin'* at the door of your refusal," he said, "while you chirped and fluttered like the bird you're named for, but really you kept dancing to the music of the 'Rich Man's Frug,' choreographed by Bob Fosse."

Frug off then. This mocking dancer and his beggar's dance wouldn't last. He wouldn't last. Everything would outlast him, especially the rich and aloof shrink, Dr. Sparrow. Since the dance floor wasn't meaningfully made for him, in the elimination dance, he made his pathetic vanishing exit. *Poof*, and, in a meaningful or non-meaningful way, for Dr. Sparrow's sake, Lover Boy danced off.

---

4   Soren Kierkegaard.

8

Dreaming Up Ways of Getting Hurt and Hurting

Those different notions of mercy and compassion led him, in part, to meet up with his mother, and to contend with her disappointments, and get her to help him, despite her usual veiled threat to tell her son where to go.

"I know what you want: like a beggar, you've come to see me. But you're ignorant."

"Of what?"

"Ignorant of the rich, the property managers, and their ignorance of the pain and the plight of the poor, like you, never to own a place, dispossessed."

"Not the stupidity of the rich?"

"That is charming, endearing even, but it is their ignorance that disgusts you."

"For you, I'm deluded, even though I live for love and work. I'm just making up stories?"

"Tell yourself another story," she said in the face of what she took to be her son's bold assertion.

"What? That you'll save me, rescue me, if only I save myself, rescue myself from my false notion of what it means to live? How bloody likely is that, do you suppose, for someone as self-destructive as I am? I don't appreciate being the designated loser in the family."

"You designated yourself, just as you volunteered to go begging, as now."

"I'm trying to figure out what the hell happened."

"What happened? You spent everything you ever made. You took without ever being able to pay anything back. You're addicted to loss is what happened to you."

"I did it to myself. Is that what you're saying?"

"Why does everything happen to you?"

"I deserve it, Mother. It couldn't happen to a nicer guy."

"What's next for you and your wife and little girls?"

"The way things are going now: we'll be making our beds in a bus shelter, or sleeping on sewer grates, in parks, under bridges or in encampments, and tent cities."

"But still, it's no from me. I can't help you anymore."

"Mother, I'm beggin' you."

"No, no, no."

He had to leave, feeling dispossessed, disinherited, unaccommodated, if for no other reason than he had to get away from volley after volley of the word being fired at him from all sides, and wounding him with friendly and unfriendly fire, especially in the back. The word (as shrapnel) was *no*, which he interpreted as *no way, no cash*, despite *the beggin' at the beggar's banquet, and beggin' at his own door, beggin' at the door of her refusal*, getting nothing from anybody, (substituting *win* with *lose*, while sticking his tongue out at his self-inflicted losses), not getting anything, not even from his own mother.

This was a desperate trick of the mind, the mental trip that seeks escape from the invisible maze, a way out in tough times, a way back to a safe haven, a sanctuary. But he couldn't go back to the past. He had to go on, even when he thought he couldn't.

"Thanks for the laughs, Mother."

9

On the Highway of Heroes

Still and all, why did he go on *beggin*? Because he was in need, and hurting, and had to. Nowhere to turn. No one else to turn to, not even creeps and freaks he used to know, like Poor Excuse, Tough Luck, and Lucky Thing. He might have to look up a guy with the moniker of Manly as in the slogan from the soap commercial. He always reeked of smelly hand soap, and was usually broke, but could always find a way of getting his hands, soap-scented, on cash, as needed. Manly and his accomplice, Kill-the-World, who never washed, were into Home Invasions, Diversion Thefts, and Counterfeiting. They left their blood stains and soapy scents everywhere they went. Where was Manly now when Lover Boy needed the bread? Where were his benefactors?

Why not work, even hurting? He had to dream up a job or jobs, not just as a hired gun, that would allow for imagination, whimsy, randomness, and especially the creative process. He was the kind of workman that wanted meaningful work. If he had to work for pay, let it be for the kind of work that was a form of play, and a way of getting paid for playing. Before he could experience such a process, or find the kind of job or work that would satisfy the creative urge and still make money, he figured that he had to choose: *yes*, he had to decide between two places, two ways of living, two schemes of life, and two women. How could he have them both, and in both ways?

Lover Boy hit the road to continue to beg in person: maybe, an old friend or two, if they remembered him. He soon found himself hitchhiking on King's Highway 2, not the Highway of Heroes, thinking he might hitch a ride. That is, if anybody would dare to stop, overcoming the fear of the spread of the Virus. Goddammit, as it turned out, believing he was heading west, distracted, confused, yet actually thumbing his way east, he was on the wrong side of the road when a semi with two Canadian flags rammed at a rebellious, red-leafed angle pulled over, and the trucker motioned for the hitchhiker to hop in.

"Take off your mask," the driver said. "Eff Trudeau."

That was how Lover Boy became part of the Freedom Convoy. Not to put too fine a point on it, he did try to explain that he wasn't actually (and not usually) that stunned about directions, but had wanted to go the other way. Yet no matter what he said, the trucker, Bob Lancaster, headed eastbound to Ottawa. Hard to believe, but Lover Boy sat back and got an earful, straight from the defiant trucker's loud mouth, about the aims of the Protest, as well as all the conspiracies of governments and pharmaceutical companies alike, and how Bill Gates was planting devices in our bodies, and all the lies about the Novel Coronavirus Covid-19. He should have jumped out when he had a chance to. It was a carnival of clichés and received ideas. Lancaster's political schtick was a carnivalesque act, freighted with conspiracy theories galore.

"Who ate the effing bat in Wuhan?" the trucker wanted to know. "Am I right?"

It wasn't only about refusing to get inoculated against Covid-19 so that truckers could cross the border between Canada and the United States, and fighting the mandates in these unprecedented and uncertain times, but also about the overthrow of the government. The truckers were organized and backed. In that context, "Eff Trudeau" made sense to Bob Lancaster, hellbent on taking back the country that he so loved. He had pulled into the little town for supplies and fuel when he had spotted the distracted hitchhiker, thumbing a ride. Lancaster immediately took the road and the ramp to Highway 401, yes, the Highway of Heroes, to try to catch up to the rest of the Freedom Convoy, and other late stragglers like himself.

To be fair or clear, Lover Boy was readying himself (and steadying his wounded body) to jump out of the cab and get back to his mission of *beggin'* when he heard pounding and thrashing coming from the trailer.

"Who's back there?" he asked.

"Why don't we take a little look-see of what's cooling in the back," Bob said. "But first, time for a piss break."

The trucker pulled the rig onto the shoulder of the highway. Then unzipped and pissed into his handy piss jug. He zipped up, unlatched and opened the door, ditched the contents of the jug, saying something about not eating the yellow snow, replaced the piss jug in its holder, jumped down, and disappeared from sight. Lover Boy wanted to seize the chance to leave, but instead, he stayed put. Who was back there? In the sideview mirror, he saw exactly who it was: *the woman with the perfect lips.* She opened the passenger side door and climbed in. She didn't seem surprised to see her lover there. Coincidence was a form of fate, or helping it along, as far as she was concerned. Lover Boy struggled to say her name: *Zouzou*. She kissed him hard on the mouth. Oh, those lips.

"You know this guy?" Bob Lancaster asked, clambering in and starting the engine.

"A lover," she said. "He's crazy about me and about my lips, aren't you, Lover Boy?"

"Zouzou Laylah, your lips, as well as other body parts, can drive any man insane."

"How did you get messed up with this trucker?" Lover Boy wanted to know.

"He picked me up at the Anti-Mask Protest at Queens Park with Anti-Vaxxers and Covid-Deniers, and here we are: off to the *Ottawa Riot.*"

Zouzou was driving Lover Boy mad, squirming next to him, and putting his hand between her thighs. She kissed him every chance she got. He realized that he couldn't get away now. He made himself responsible for Zouzou and her perfect lips, especially with the trucker repeatedly eyeballing her or parts of her.

"Where are you going, lover?" she whispered into his ear.

"The wrong way," Lover Boy said. "I'm supposed to be going in the other direction. Turns out I was out of my head, and thumbing a ride on the wrong side of the road. I should have been on the northside, and not the southside."

"Why didn't you say so?" Bob Lancaster broke out.

"Where *were* you heading?" Zouzou asked Lover Boy.

"To deliver a letter, and then on my way to see *you* in the Big City."

"Here I am, Lover Boy. Saved you the fare, money being what it is these days: tight."

"A coincidence."

"Coincidence is fate sometimes. All roads lead to Zouzou's lips."

"Does that go for truckers as well?" Lancaster had to find out.

Zouzou wouldn't say. She kissed Lover Boy instead and kept holding on. *Tight.*

The trucker controlled the tunes playing on the radio. Zouzou was singing along, coaxing Lover Boy to sing. He hesitated until "That's

alright mama" came on. At that point, he did his best Elvis impersonation. He didn't like most pop music, and when he was young, he hated it, going against the trends of the times, because it meant so much to
kids of his generation, but he had made an exception for Elvis Presley.

The trucker went wild, as Zouzou moved her hips back and forth,
dancing her ass off on the front seat. They kept singing until, catching
up, they joined the other trucks on the highway in the army of semis
that formed the Freedom Convoy. They weren't in the first ranks that
had already established a base in Ottawa. Rather, they were part of the
influx and wave in the lagging days that followed. It wasn't long before
Lancaster, Lover Boy and Zouzou were shouting at each other in the
cab, half-jesting in mock-political-pundit-style, as if Rex Morphy and
other ranters were truck drivers. It was all about the protest.

"Now if you're prepared to go all the way," Lancaster was saying.

"Smash everything," Lover Boy said. "Destroy it all. Burn it down.
But you're going to get your teeth kicked in when you get there. You
can't block the border towns without getting it. And what with the
hell the fat orange man is unleashing south of the border, we're likely
doomed."

"You're scarier than the leaders of the Freedom Convoy. They just
want to hang Trudeau, while you want to destroy everything."

"Jack (Lover Boy) Cade on the Barricades."

"Come and lie down with me," Zouzou said.

"I would, but I'm driving," the trucker said.

"I was referring to my Lover Boy," she said.

"Where do we lie down?" he asked.

"The trailer," she said. "Bob has fixed everything up with mattresses
and supplies."

"There'll be no lying down or stopping until we reach our destina-
tion," the trucker said. "And then, I'll tell you who gets to lie down."

That was the killer moment when Lover Boy knew he had to get
Zouzou, despite her giggle-fest, away from Bob Lancaster, to free her
from that freak, no joke, and to extricate his own sorry ass, too, from
the trucker's menacing freakshow.

10

Freedom

Four hours later, Bob Lancaster successfully slammed his semi into Ottawa and heroically butted the monstrous truck up against other massive rigs in the siege and takeover of Ottawa. Not far from Parliament Hill, the freedom protest was in full swing. Hundreds of vehicles revved their engines, and then roared and honked their displeasure at Prime Minister Justin Trudeau. This was not an anti-vaccination movement any longer, but rather, a freedom movement. The protesters said so with calls for Trudeau to get the hell out. They denounced him as a corrupt politician, liar, dictator, and a privileged, arrogant, entitled, poster boy for effing *woke,* and the ideals of *woke-ism.*

"How else, besides revolutionary actions, can we reclaim justice from those that hate our values and our guts as much as we hate theirs?"

In rage and revolt, big rigs were steadfastly blocking access to the downtown core. While they outfaced Parliament Hill, workers in soup kitchens and restaurants faced harassment with protesters demanding to be fed for free.

"A protester deserves free food, don't he?"

Some truckers were shitting on front lawns.

"Well, they have to take a shit somewhere, don't they?"

Did they expect losers like Lover Boy to scoop up their daily turds? The best or most revealing line that came out of the anti-*vaxxers* dealt with the common good: that they weren't prepared *to sacrifice their bodies for it.* Blaring horns deafened the citizens. Protesters drank and danced on the Tomb of the Unknown Soldier. Posters went up with upside down Canadian flags on the statue of Terry Fox.

"Terry Fox?"

Did they give a damn anymore about old heroes? Trucks blocked the emergency department at the hospital, and had to be towed, if the authorities could get a towing company to do the towing. Only certain media were given access to the spokespersons of the protest. Other media were forbidden to get anywhere near them. Police presence was pitifully slight, necessarily with the finite number of cops in the city. White nationalists spoke. Islamophobes spoke their piece, too, advocating anything but peace. How many protesters were there? Estimates suggested 5,000 to 15,000 in the initial days. Protests were disruptive. Officials were outnumbered, even overwhelmed. Protesters were getting dug in: no retreat, no surrender. *GoFundMe* had raised millions of dollars, mostly American, for their use. This resulted in vandalism, hate, violence, and fun. Yet personal stories had it that it was the best time of their lives. To Lover Boy, it was noise, the kind that defied and puzzled the intellect.

Lover Boy did get to sleep with Zouzou in the back of the rig. She was all over him. He enjoyed more than her lips. Did he think of his wife and kids? Not sure. To think of them would require him, in his pleasure, to think of the town where he had taken his family to live. He had abandoned them there. He would rather think of the Big City. That meant thinking, and not just dreaming, of Zouzou. She was with him now, anyway, and she was a moveable feast.

One night, in a dispute about who was going to sleep with her, Lover Boy got into a violent confrontation with Bob Lancaster. Lover Boy would have won the fight but for the fact that the trucker used a tire iron to try to thrash him. When he heard Lancaster say: "Jesus Morphy, fight back," Lover Boy caved and let the trucker wail away with deadly blows.

"Why didn't you defend yourself?" Zouzou demanded, sticking Lancaster with a knife in the back of his right thigh to stop him from killing her lover.

"I felt that I deserved a good thrashing," Lover Boy said. "It's what was supposed to happen next, I guess. I was supposed to get bashed."

Zouzou tended his wounds. From then on, she did her level best to keep him away from Lancaster. Lover Boy and Zouzou took the money with them: money that belonged to the trucker. They didn't know how long it would take him to figure it out. That is, figure out the theft and the thieves' whereabouts hidden among the other protesters. After the beating, wished for, postponed, carried out, deserved or not, and the theft, the couple hooked up with another trucker named Joe Bucco.

"They say my name means 'hole' in Italian," he said. "Not true: that would be *buco*? But not *buco di culo*, as they say on my side of an Italian card game. I have an asshole, but I'm not one. My name refers to the mouth."

This mouthy Bucco, asshole or not, let them stay in his truck, especially when he was enjoying himself so much at the winter barbecue. He was having a ball standing up to, and outfacing, the police.

"This is the best time of my life," Bucco said, "no matter who is behind it, and backing it. The effing Pandemic, real or not, has stolen my time and my freedom. It's left a big hole in my life and my place in history. So, fighting for freedom gives it back to me: the missing piece. I'm helping to make history."

"Thanks for taking us in," Zouzou said. "This is our honeymoon."

"A stolen one," Lover Boy said with black eyes and a fat lip.

"What?"

"We're not married, you see, not to each other," Zouzou said.

"Right, right, a stolen honeymoon during a riot," Bucco said, "married, but not to each other. Does it get any better than that? I met a lady with *bouncy-castle* breasts last night. We have a date later at the Bouncy Castle. The kids had better watch out. Bouncy, bouncy."

They never really saw much of Bucco after that, and were glad of it. While he went off to the pig roast and stripped down to jump into the outdoor sauna, despite the winter weather, Zouzou tried to get Lover Boy interested in what was going on around them. What was going on?

Though he couldn't stand the noise and the brutality, he did tune in to the wild speeches, the hysterical rhetoric, and the fractured discourse. It sounded like a yelling match between shouting choruses. He began calling out, as well, shouting slogans, and soon started making speeches himself, off-the-cuff remarks that he thought had wit and edge. Did he believe he was speaking up for the working man? Who knew that he was a great improviser? He would out-rant the ranters and outshout the shouters. If he heard political talk that he took to be crazy, his own kind of anarchistic talk would become crazier than what he had heard. If he heard the speakers pushing right-wing views, with reference to fake news and conspiracy theories, he went farther right, more so than anyone could imagine. It wasn't long before he started receiving attention, and then getting envelopes with cash and cards loaded with funds that he could spend on anything he liked. He was being backed, bankrolled, and sponsored. He soon realized that he could burn the *beggin'* letter in the fires set by the protesters. Funnily enough, he now had more than adequate funds, easy money in envelopes, to finance his own schemes. Lover Boy was also getting the attention of the police and the press.

Ottawa was under siege. What had happened to the Omicron Variant, to Covid-19? The last weekend in January, the horns blared day and night. It was so cold that he and Zouzou huddled close to each other just for a little warmth. There was talk of staying in a hotel with the bill to be covered by the protest organizers that turned out to be just talk.

The perception of some was that these acts were part of an insurrection and even the beginning of the new world order. Hadn't they seen something like this in America on January 6, staged or not? How do you silence the honking horns? How do you deal with mobs? Would injunctions ever work? Class-action lawsuits: how would they succeed if the police couldn't control the crowds or make arrests? Some of the residents felt threatened, blocked. Where were their rights to law, peace, and order?

Teamsters Canada denied any association with the Freedom Convoy. How many of them were certified truckers? To some, hate was on display. To others, the working of freedom. Protesters had barbecues. They played the national sport, hockey, anywhere they could. Bouncy castles were set up for their kids. New alliances were formed. Conservative, NDP, and the Bloc were welcomed in, but not the Liberals. The talk was increasingly more violent. Was this an attempt to overthrow the government?

"No mandates."

"And NO Trudeau."

The word *siege* was being bandied about. Protesters still outnumbered the cops. How long would the *fun* and the *occupation* last? Was this an emergency, a threat to national security? Not to mention border blockades. Demands were made to meet with scientists to declare Covid-19 a Hoax. Was this anti-government noise? Anti-authoritarian tribalism? Some wanted the government dissolved. That went viral as part of a media circus.

"You're with me now," Zouzou said, "but you're thinking of her… and *them*."

"Just thinking," he said, "about the grief that is coming. I'm here with you, but we're going to get the shit beat out of us."

"We're winning, Lover Boy. We won't give up. Look at us. We're freedom-loving. When the losers win, the world is upside down."

"Who's really in control?"

"The ones speaking up for us."

"The ones you see and hear, but behind them are the ones you never see. You just feel the presence of their money and their dark ideologies."

"They're giving us that money for the long haul. For our freedom."

"Freedom can also be just another illusion."

"What's happened to you, Lover Boy?"

"Trucker beat the hell out of me."

"No, I mean, with all this anarchy and violence, and *grief*, as you said."

"It's the Pandemic, lockdown, masks, mandates, the Vax: they've brought out something strange in me. No, they've stolen something from me, something that will never be replaced."

"The worst in you?"

"The feeling of nothing," he said, "emptiness, nihilism, subversion, hate, and the need to hate, to make excuses, justifications, especially for myself. But I just want to work."

"I love you, Lover Boy. I'm sure your wife and kids love you, too."

"You all love a loser then."

"You *want* to lose. You want to get beaten up. Do you want to get killed? With that look in your black-and-blue eyes, what could you possibly be thinking about?"

"Never throw your gun away."

"What gun?"

"The one I threw away."

"You would've shot him?"

"We'll never know."

"Glad you threw it away, Lover Boy. Get rid of the hate, too, and anger. Let me help you."

She touched his swollen face. Went out and gathered handfuls of snow. Then packed it on his puffy eyes and scarred mouth.

"We can have a good time while this Carnival lasts," she said. "The honeymoon is not over yet."

"Not until the government declares a state of emergency," he said. "At some point in the future, what's happened to us has to be comprehended in detail. You'll see the siege and the stolen honeymoon will come to a bitter end at the same time."

Prime Minister Trudeau invoked the Emergencies Act with the power to go after the money, bring in law enforcement, make arrests, compel tow truck companies to provide tow trucks, tow the big rigs, and take back the city and the blocked border crossings. Nobody would forget what he did. Who could ever forgive him? Protesters would haunt him and hound him for the rest of his days. That was what had happened to the Protest and to their Stolen Honeymoon. Funnily enough, and with mirthless, ungrateful laughter, that was what had happened as well to their sense of *freedom*.

11

Dream of Disappearing

He was dreaming about Priscilla and their daughters, Ana and Lina. They didn't know where he was, unless they had caught a glimpse of him in the news footage from Ottawa. Priscilla liked Ottawa. They had visited the city on a number of occasions. She loved skating on the frozen Rideau Canal in winter, and checking out the Parliament Buildings in the spring. Lover Boy stopped dreaming of her skating as he saw what some were calling *extremist* action unfolding on the Hill and in the Convoy occupying the city.

The dismantling of the Protest/Insurrection/Whatever-It-Was began around the 17th of February with the arrest of protesters, towing of vehicles, and tearing down of blockades. By the 20th, the police had secured the streets. Were Anti-Riot Weapons discharged at the crowds? Some said so. Others said a woman had been knocked down and trampled by a horse. Denials and accusations went back and forth. Phone lines were jammed for emergency services. With the new powers under the Emergencies Act, the authorities could follow the paper/money trail. Did they shut down accounts? Some claimed so. Others denied it. By the 21st, the city seemed abandoned, a ghost town. Trudeau was denounced as a dictator and a coward. He was depicted in cartoons as hiding out, a *frightened idiot*, as some called him, from the truckers.

Though Lover Boy and Zouzou were both arrested and detained under the Act, she was released shortly after her detention. She had no political affiliations, and no prior police record. She did get a lawyer with Joe Bucco's help. As for Lover Boy, he was booked to face a judge owing to the speeches and the evidence captured by cameras and cell phones. They confiscated the money he carried on him. What had happened to his *beggin' letter*? Who was ever going to stand hearing him out after this, anyway?

In what turned out to be a *lousy* defense, he said to the police that he was poking fun at the rhetoric: dark humour with a sense of irony were behind his seemingly sinister words, in his brand of nihilism, and anti-government tirades. He said that he found the northern *insurrection* laughable, a political farce that attempted to imitate the perversity of January 6 south of the border, another political carnival.

"I'm at a low point in my life," he said, trying to smirk. "I'm raging against everything, far left and far right. Today, everybody is trying to destroy or cancel everybody else with one conspiracy theory against another. We've entered into a time of mass hysteria and mass delusion. Irony is the only way to keep sane. How else can we fight against universal Trumpism, the political clown show, the carnival of intolerance and hate, disinformation, misinformation, resentment and fear? You can't pay your bills these days. Sometimes, you can't breathe from the Virus or from the mask. You hold and save your breath for death. You can't buy a house, or even pay for groceries, let alone medicines. You often see the homeless living on the streets, in encampments, under bridges or collapsed in front of methadone clinics. You ask yourself: 'What the hell is going on? Why have we failed? Where can we turn?' So why did I lose? Why can't losers win? Why did I fail? What I ended up wanting was to get thrashed, to be humiliated, to get kicked and punched, to be punished, because, *because* I deserved it? No, because I was owed at least that much. Violence was the only way out. I started talking after years of silence, gagging on my own inability to say what the hell I was feeling and thinking. When I began talking, I couldn't stop spewing my misery and contempt, spitting up my blues. I was like a channel for all the shit and filth, faithlessness and mindlessness I was forced to listen to, and respond to. I was a mouthpiece for my time. This loser was trying to tell everybody the history of failure and disappointment in the face of greed and vaccination, lockdown and isolation. The world had taken something from me for two years. The hole it made in me was huge, a gaping wound that would never heal. It was as empty of meaning as it was full of shit. That's what you heard, or heard tell of me during the Protest. I was clowning around: *a Clown of the Revolution.*"

"A comedian of the Freedom Convoy?" the investigator/interrogator demanded. "Do you think it's funny, the violence, the destruction?

"Funny that I'm here," he said. "Yes, a dupe, an idiot."

"A fool?"

"A failed comedian," he said.

"Laughing at the police? A political joker? I'd like to wipe that smirk off your face."

"A political comic doing his campy routine in self-mockery, in self-derision, and derision of everything he sees. Is laughing at myself a crime?"

"It shows contempt, especially in front of a judge and jury."

He had to call Priscilla to help him make it through the legal process, maybe with Tad's financial aid, in the guise of political clowning around, and to help set him free. He'd have a record. She ended up borrowing money from her brother, something she had sworn she would never do again.

"Where's your mistress?" she had asked him.

"I don't know," he said. "She's disappeared."

He didn't want to be snide, but he was. He dreamed of Zouzou disappearing with either Lancaster or Bucco, but couldn't decide on which option was the most farcical. She was likely in somebody's truck, dancing in the front seat, or lying on a mattress in the trailer, bound to some unknown somewhere right now. She was a survivor. Imagine if women like Zouzou didn't exist. He was sure she would find a way of dropping back into his poor excuse for a life once she got herself together. For her, the Freedom Convoy would probably become the story of her life. It certainly wasn't for Jack (Lover Boy) Cade. The story of his life still had to be written.

He now had a police record with suspicions of being an agitator/subversive/traitor/clown. He felt bad about losing the money, but had to get back to finding his way forward. Despite his jeers and sneers, instead of disappearing, he had to find work. This was just another kick in the pants, a political punch in the face, a pratfall. He hated it and loved it at the same time. He hated the context of his punishment, but, even as he cringed at the thought, he loved the fact that he'd been punished again. Did he, in some farcical way, appear to disappear, and, in a weird twist, just as the money had vanished, win again, at least bragging rights, by losing once again?

12

Figuring Everything Out

Once released, trying to figure everything out, the first thing he saw was Priscilla and the kids standing in the snow outside the Detention Centre. It had been a snowy ordeal for them to get there. The police removed his handcuffs and released him from custody. The release came with conditions, along with a record. The kids cheered, as if he had won a game, and ran over to see their dad. He knelt down to hug both girls, but refused to look up at Priscilla. She didn't say a word. She had called a cab. The cabby waited for them to climb inside. Priscilla asked the cab driver to take the family to the bus terminal. She had bought tickets for the homeward trip. He sat with the eldest child, while Priscilla cuddled the youngest in her arms. Their mother had snacks and drinks for the little ones. Their dad wouldn't accept anything to eat or drink. He was already dreaming about what would happen next. How would it all turn out? After the long bus ride, they got off on the northside of King's Highway 2, not the southside from where he had hitched a ride to Ottawa. It wasn't far at all from their rented house.

Priscilla prepared something for the kids before putting them to bed. Lover Boy accepted a coffee and sipped it, standing looking out at the street from the front window. He had to start over. He told Priscilla that he would take her and the girls to the Big City to spend some time there together. Maybe, it would help them to decide to move back: a reality check of sorts against the haziness of nostalgia. He tried to make Priscilla laugh with his comic routine about the horrors of a small town. She laughed, but with tears in her eyes.

"We could get out of here," Priscilla said, "and pay rent on *one* place, not two. We can start over. You've got to figure it out, Jack."

If only he had slept with her, he might have felt better about what was going on. What was going on? Again, he felt fazed by the decision he was forced to make. He slept on the couch. Next day, he kept his promise to visit the Big City with the family. They left Weenie, their dog, with an obliging neighbour. Priscilla used her credit card to buy Go Train tickets. The kids wore masks, so did Priscilla. Lover Boy let his mask hang down over his ear. The kids found him funny, and told him so.

They did visit, and stayed in a largely empty apartment, remembering the places they used to go. They went to the park and to the Village. When the kids wanted an ice cream cone, Priscilla told them it was too cold for ice cream. They visited Casa Loma, not far from the apartment, and the Spadina House Museum blanketed in snow where the children used to play when they were very young. They wanted to head down to the Harbourfront and then to Centre Island, but it was getting late and too cold for an adventure.

When they got back into the apartment building, Lover Boy spotted someone hiding in the hallway, crouched down by his apartment door. He confronted him, and got into a dispute with the homeless man, flushed him out and made him scurry down the stairs. Lover Boy followed him only to see him squatting down on the lower level.

"The apartment building is overrun by intruders, freaks and creeps," he said.

By living there, something or somebody always pissed him off. He was seldom, if ever, without entanglements, and a shitload of trouble, fuss or bother. One time, he began a feud with an old couple that lived downstairs, directly under his apartment. The old guy (his name was Ray Fango) had long white hair that looked like a dandelion gone-to-seed. Ray never shut up: talked day and night, mostly at the top of his lungs. He fought a pitched and vicious battle with plates, pots and pans, losing every match. He stomped around the place with what sounded like cowboy boots with spurs.

He must have fallen a lot, too, or thrown his body on the floor with heavy thuds. He had the TV on non-stop, and the radio blasted the airwaves and the other tenants' eardrums 24/7. The loudmouth had it in for his old lady, (according to Priscilla, her name was Nella), railing against her, calling her names, and every kind of bitch or witch, and generally trying to straighten her out about life and the hell of a mess the world was in. The old girl looked much younger than he did. She always dressed like women half her age, or half her *rage*, to hear her shouting. Priscilla told her husband that the old girl had been a stripper back in the day, maybe the Victory and Burlesque. Ray was always throwing shade on her for it.

In the past, some of the old folks complained about noise made by young people disturbing their peace and quiet. Now, younger people like Lover Boy had to yell at them for the endless noise coming from their apartment. Nella had once told Priscilla that they had an infestation of flies. Ray hated flytraps or simple swatters. He went after the swarm with a bat, a cricket bat.

When the old man tried to change bulbs, Lover Boy could hear the whole farce and slapstick routine, including silent film music. The bulb would fall and smash to smithereens. The old man would fall off his stepladder with a crash and bang. That was how it sounded. Lover Boy went down once to talk to Ray, and even offered to help him. Ray told him to go away, and went for his bat. Lover Boy resorted to pounding the walls or stomping his heel on the floor (their ceiling) to get them to shut up and turn off the incessant racket coming from below. He had to shut them up, didn't he? The girls couldn't sleep for the noise. They retaliated by hitting their ceiling (Lover Boy's floor) with a broom handle or cane, if they could reach on the stepladder, each time the girls cried, or the dog barked, or ran around.

He found the old man in the alley one night with the garbage, the rats, raccoons and pigeons. Old man Ray was taking swigs from all but empty booze bottles before throwing them into the recycling bin. He noticed Lover Boy, turned around, and half ran away. Then stumbled and fell, and just lay there. Lover Boy tried to help the old guy up, but he twisted out of Lover Boy's grip, and told him to go piss up a rope, and took off.

The feud lasted until one of the oldsters stopped talking altogether. Priscilla felt sorry for them, insisting that Lover Boy had harassed them needlessly. She said she hated his aggression towards the old couple.

"Better than being an informant and lodging a complaint," he said. "Complainers and whiners make me sick."

She said he wasn't yelling at his wife: he was an old actor, rehearsing and reciting his lines aloud. Lover Boy said he hardly cared who he was. Too bad he wasn't a mime, practising the art of silence. Since he wasn't, Lover Boy just wanted to get back at him. In those days, it came down to revenge. He couldn't simply walk away, could he? If he didn't retaliate, he would regret it. They were old. They had to die off sooner or later. One of Lover Boy's criminal friends once called not avenging yourself "the regret of non-violence." Later on, maybe too late to do any good, Lover Boy learned to shun and snub those that had wronged him. He resented it only to become a collector of grievances. It was always the same: there was always trouble.

Even going back to the apartment was fraught. Though he realized that "you can't go home again," he would not/could not make the decision about abandoning the apartment, not yet. Instead, he would visit the people he had known in the past to see if they would give him a handout. The trip ended badly, and Priscilla, Ana and Lina went back to the little town without him. He stayed on, trying to promise that he needed only a few days to figure things out.

No sooner had he watched his wife and kids descending the stairs than he saw Zouzou with Joe Bucco in tow climbing up to the 4th floor. Had they seen Priscilla and the children leaving the building? Had the others seen Zouzou and Bucco entering? Of course, Zouzou had made it back after the Freedom Convoy debacle to return to the apartment that Lover Boy kept, in part, for her sake. Bucco was bounding behind her. What had the irrepressible Zouzou promised him for the ride he had given her?

"Lover Boy," she said. "You knew I'd be here sooner or later. I willed you to be here, and here you are."

"Ciao, Cade?" Bucco said, as red-cheeked as a circus clown. "Released, I see. You've got a criminal record now. You're a gangster."

Was he pleased or disappointed to see Lover Boy?

"We're veterans of the revolution, aren't we? Zouzou promised me something."

"Something to eat," she said, "without fringe benefits. (Zouzou laughed.) I'm saving myself for you, Lover Boy. Let's go in and figure everything out."

"So, is this where the funny revenge story really begins?"

In a group hug, they kissed him, and went in.

PART TWO

1

The Prizefighter

"And we get them [moments of vivid excitement] from work and love. By work I don't mean shovelling coal or teaching children, I mean work which gives you a conspicuous place in the world. And by love I don't mean marriage or friendship, I mean independent love which stops when the excitement stops. Perhaps I've surprised you by putting work and love in the same category, but both are ways of mastering other people."
—Alasdair Gray, *Lanark*

As part of the figuring, he figured that he had no money, was up to his eyeballs, no, his eyebrows, in debt and shit, in a daze, as he said, and simply wanting to survive. He had to fight, in a weird sense, by not fighting at all. This kind of contradiction helped him to reject everything for the time being. No *beggin'*. No appeals.

"Reject those that reject you. Tell them to get out. Shun them. Move. Move on. Stick and move, like a prizefighter. Jab, jab, stick and move. Keep dancing on the tips of your toes. That's the way to fight without fighting. No more dope-a-rope either, if it comes to that. By punching yourself in the face, you win in the last round with a knockout punch, beaten by yourself, but still not out for the count by anyone else's fist."

By deliberately losing, he reasoned, seeing the matter from his own angle, he would win. Sort of. That is, by not wanting to win, he had beaten others at their own merciless game. One thing was sure: he needed time to get it together. That was what he had said to Priscilla, watching her going down those sad stairs. No, just move on. Survive.

Arrive alive. The dream wasn't over, was it? The new city had to be dreamed up in a new dream of a re-imagined life. Both city and town needed a rewrite. His conception of them had to be written over again. Do you write a new place by yourself? Or do you co-author it? Who knew? Making it new was the point.

Bucco knew a lot about making money under the table. He referred Lover Boy to a certain Shaydon, a shady man for whom he had worked before in his bizarre gambling enterprise. This Shaydon had given Bucco cash on several occasions for carrying out unspecified but laughable work, the nature of which always baffled Bucco, but made Shaydon rich and even richer.

"But you're smarter than me, Lover Boy," Joe Bucco said. "You'll be able to figure out what Shaydon really does for a living, and do better than I ever did."

Though he felt numb, Lover Boy listened to Bucco, and agreed to go to the address that the trucker passed along to him.

"I'll call ahead, and let Shaydon's people know that you're coming," Bucco said. "Whatever you do, just play along. See cruelty as kindness, weirdness as normal, and Shaydon's oddball games as total reality."

Lover Boy went down to a place in the Distillery District. When he buzzed, he was let in. This, that, and he was telling his story to a short, squat man, dressed in an electric blue suit and yellow tie. In the room was a card table and two chairs. Once introductions were over with, Shaydon asked him the following question:

"What's your real story?"

Lover Boy hesitated at first and then launched in.

"So, this thing that happened in Ottawa," he spluttered, "is the story I'm telling lately."

He told his tale of unemployment to go on with, and maybe, to see how much cash he could get from the listener. Was Shaydon listening for key words and phrases, certain qualities in the storyteller, to determine his true worth and value, and how he could make use of him? Would Lover Boy's version of events result in getting some of Shaydon's money? Would the story and the way it was being told help him to survive a little bit longer?

"What do you want now after the attempted insurrection, the so-called fight for freedom?" Shaydon wanted to know. "Let me guess: *cash*."

"Cash," Lover Boy said. "Willing to work for it. What do you need from me?"

"Your body," Shaydon said. "I'm not saying your soul, not yet. I'm not saying your mind as well."

"Not yet?"

"Body, mind and soul are worth paying for, if you're selling."

"What do I have to do? What do I have to sell?"

"Your ability to *take* it."

"Take what? A life? Other people's property?"

"A good beating, so that bets can be placed on the guy getting bashed and thrashed, and be able to dish it out, when asked to. Game?"

"Let's play. I'm playing to lose, right? It's fixed, and in your favour."

"We're not just *playing*, but for keeps. I'll give you a little taste of what's in store."

Shaydon withdrew a wad of bills, and set the money on the table in front of the player.

"A blood-sport?"

Shaydon rapped his fat, white knuckles on the table, mimicking a mobster. A guy came in as if passing through the wall instead of through a door. When he stepped up, he gave Lover Boy a hard and piercing body blow to the kidneys. Then seemed to disappear back through the wall.

"You want to beat the shit out of me?" he asked. "Everybody does already. You want to watch me suffer? Is that what makes you hard?"

"I can watch anybody suffer whenever I like," Shaydon said. "But how much can you take, and how much can I make from it?"

"I don't get to fight back?"

"No point. Bucco told me you like getting slapped around."

Lover Boy didn't fight back. He couldn't. He was trapped, desperately wanting the cash just sitting there in stacks on the table. Cash for pain? Was that the right description for this working arrangement? He kept his hands by his sides, shrugging off the pain. He had nearly buckled over and almost blacked out. His ribs were no doubt messed up. His bruised body was already a mess.

"Bloodied, bruised, messed up," Shaydon said. "Bandages will be useless. Your face will be swollen, your nose likely broken."

"Again," Lover Boy said. "It's already broken."

Next to come in was the trucker who had broken his nose again. Bob Lancaster wasted no time in laying into him with arms flailing.

"Where's Zouzou?" he kept saying. "She's *my* woman."

"She's *nobody's* woman," Lover Boy whispered.

"Where's my money?" Lancaster demanded. "It's my money. I'll keep coming after you for it."

"I see that you two know each other. Lancaster works for me. As for you, blood will be dripping all over the bloody place," Shaydon shot out, thinking he wasn't being believed, "from your mouth and the wounds to the head and every wound in your body, and you'll be spitting out your teeth."

"Do it," he said. "I'm nothing. Nothing."

Lancaster had another go at him, his comical victim, with brutal kicks to his right leg, demanding to know where Zouzou and his money were hiding out. That was when others came in and jumped in, trying to kick Lover Boy's head in, sticking him with a knife, but just to cut him and not kill him yet. The hysterical thing was that he wouldn't let go of his grotesque silence. He deserved it, the beating, for all the hurt he had ever caused others. He just lay there, all beat up, and thinking they were going to finish him off. He was on his back now with his arms at his sides, in surrender, and then Shaydon took the wad of bills and let them cascade onto Lover Boy's bloodied face and wounded upper body. Lancaster and the gang took off at Shaydon's command.

"I'm not picking them up," Lover Boy said.

"Good for you," Shaydon said. "It's only the start. You're a born victim, a masochist. You hate yourself. So, it'll make it a good bet to see how much you can stand to suffer. The blood will be yours."

Blood, for sure, was his, blood of a working man, but what part of this ordeal was a sport?

"Get up. Somebody will pick up your winnings for you. That'll help to keep what's left of your dignity, won't it?"

He had to stand up, unaided. Lover Boy fought his need to stay down on the floor, and slowly and mechanically made it to his feet. Shaydon gestured for him to move to the wall. A part of it became a door through which Shaydon shoved Lover Boy's body, and where he found himself in a dark room: a screening room. A large screen descended from the ceiling.

"Watch," Shaydon said, "even with half-closed eyelids. You're not eating or drinking for the next while. You'll relieve yourself when I say so. What I'm telling you to do is just *watch*. These are classics."

He was referring to classic bouts, famous fights from boxing history with no sound or commentary. Lover Boy was already half-dead.

How much of this could he take? Shaydon's place was a gambler's paradise, catering to special tastes that went far beyond cards and games of chance. Lover Boy would have to take as much punishment as Shaydon's gamblers, goons and flunkeys would dole out. For him, it was about the money, and a kind of penance that he thought, for his own ironic reasons, he had to do. Didn't he deserve a good beating for the way his wife and kids had walked down the apartment stairs, leaving him to watch them in bewildered silence? Somebody had to atone for their tears. Since he needed to be hurt and wanted it, he simply waited for it to happen.

On the screen, he saw Jack Dempsey, Joe Louis, Rocky Marciano, George Chuvalo, Joe Frasier, George Foreman, Mohammad Ali, and other boxers. He felt each and every body-blow and uppercut. He identified, not with the winner of the match, but the loser. He was the eternal loser. When the screen went dead, he was confronted by yelling and screaming until a spotlight revealed that he wasn't alone: a fighter stood in front of him, posturing up. A bell rang. A chorus of voices called out:

"Hit him. Again. Again. Kill him."

When he was beaten to a pulp, he didn't even raise his arms to protect his swollen face. He stood bent double, waiting to pass out. When he came to, he was sitting at the table, slumped over in a chair.

"You pissed off the fighter something awful," Shaydon said.

Something awful also buzzed in Lover Boy's brain. He struggled to keep his eyes open. Then recalled a voice saying:

"Get him out of there, little loser. Right, right, he thinks he can take it. Take *this*."

"You took it," Shaydon said, stacking bills in front of the loser. "You endured it, withstood it, and prevailed. That's how losers win. The betting went as I had wanted it to go. I knew it would, thanks to you. You didn't even try to defend yourself. You didn't stick and move. But it was what you kept saying under your breath that sustained you, and even though the other guy pummeled you, thrashed you, you stung him with your weird inaction, and fooling around, and the wickedly funny *words* of a sarcastic, victimized son-of-a-bitch."

2

Not Much

He'd been talking, apparently, while being defeated. It wouldn't be enough to survive the beatings, would it? Talking, he meant. No, it wouldn't. He knew why.

"Is that all you got?" he kept saying, despite himself.

Was there anything more pathetic than a luckless loser using words against fists? It was like a professional boxer beating up a standup comedian. His taunts and jests were nothing but trash talk. Where was everybody while he got the shit beaten out of him? Where were they now? Waiting, watching him getting killed from wherever they were? Still, where were Priscilla, Zouzou, the kids, Bucco and so on, when he was bleeding all over the place, even as he sat slumped in the chair that seemed to hold him down with the gravitational pull of locks and chains? In his predicament, how could he be expected to figure everything out, let alone anything? His mouth seemed to work independently of his will.

What was he after: money, pleasure, power, meaning? Lover Boy had to have his say. He had to speak his truth, no matter how inconvenient it was. He was being used for the pleasure of others. A loser was/is a loser, but did they have power over him if he gave over to the punishment? How had he let himself be used by other losers, nonentities, that likely needed a good shit-kicking themselves, but for their money? How had he let himself be pushed this far by the son-of-a-bitch that was playing with him now? Why had Lover Boy let himself be taken for the sad clown he had become, to be tortured and almost killed, or at least mutilated, nearly massacred, for what he had done or not done?

What had he done? Stolen somebody else's woman, Zouzou? Or insulted his wife by cheating on her? Their living together was a bad romance. She was too clingy, too intense. He hadn't exactly dumped her, just let things cool off, and fade out. You can't be expected to return every call and answer every text and email with so much to do in city life.

Was that enough to get a man tortured and killed? Something had to happen, right? Somebody had to pay when the time came for a reckoning. Everybody knew that something had to go down. It didn't exactly go down that night. He was still alive, but barely. No one tended to his wounds. Shaydon gawked at him, and said:

"You didn't get knocked down even as they jumped you, like one of the great boxers, Gratiano, say."

He told Lover Boy to ditch the martyr act.

"You know why you're here, just as you knew you'd be arrested in Ottawa. No freedom then. No mercy now. You'll never go home again. Not from here, not from anywhere. That's the meaning of your sad life."

"Damn me," he said. "And goddamn you, Shaydon, if that's your real and ugly name."

"You're *nobody*," Shaydon said, "with black eyes and a broken nose."

He told Lover Boy he was no-man, the last man on the earth, and the loneliest in the city or any little town. He said that he was a *nothing*. No passport, no papers, a hopeless case. *Martyr* was how he put it when he mentioned Lover Boy's lost dignity.

"Dignity, my ass."

They would find his feet in his shit-soled shoes washed up on the lakeshore, and nobody would give a flying fuck. He knew now where he was, and what his insignificant position was in the extreme, stripped down and essentially bare.

Shaydon sat secure in his position and place, powerful in perpetuity. Amen. Stacks of money formed his defenses, his barricades. Lover Boy stared at him, contemplating revolt, a supreme effort to smash everything and get away. He eyed him with half-closed eyes and then spoke up.

"It's over," he said.

Shaydon laughed.

"Yeah," Lover Boy said, imitating him. "Real funny."

He called him an asshole, and let it slip out that he hated the money. He just wanted out of there.

"It must be very rewarding," he said, "like betting on a dying man, by first watching him suffer, like some kind of sadistic gag."

Shaydon kept laughing at the gagman, trying not to gloat too much, but really enjoying it, Lover Boy could tell.

"No, I'm glad for you, Shaydon. I am."

His mouth was doing all the talking, as if it had a mind of its own. It did, because it bled. His seething anger was white hot. He could go scorched earth, but this time his heat was a controlled burn.

"You're a buffoon," Shaydon said.

"No denying it," Lover Boy said.

For him, life was a joke. He made another joke about it, as if doing standup.

"We can forget about the whole thing, the beatings, the sadistic torture."

"Just forget about it?" Shaydon asked.

"The obligations, the duties," Lover Boy said, "the rights you bought and own, and just walk away. People do walk away, no hard feelings about the shitshow."

"No money, either," Shaydon said. "You'll get nothing."

Not exactly nothing when two dogs of an unknown breed ran into the room with the ferocity of killers. They attacked him still sitting in the chair. They tried to maul him, tearing into him, dragging him to the ground. He managed to grab the ears of one of the animals. Was this the end?

Shaydon called off the dogs. The attack dogs disengaged, and ran off, as if through the walls.

"How much longer could you have withstood that?" Shaydon asked.

When Lover Boy said, *"Not much,"* without looking up, the old man said:

"Thought so, funnyman."

"I'm done with your abuse."

"Walk out, if you can, Cade, but you don't get the cash. You get nothing."

Shaydon went to the window, drew aside the curtain, and gestured to his goons to let the victim pass. They let him go, penniless. He was beaten and broke, but free. He had taken it, and not inflicted pain on anyone, not even the dogs. He breezed by Shadon's men, and walked out into a city snowstorm. The cold wind dealt with the burning and stinging of his many wounds. When he heard someone calling his name, at first, he refused to see who it was. Then he realized it was Zouzou. She had persuaded Bucco to tell her where Lover Boy had gone. She got him back safely to the apartment where she stretched him out on the couch and took care of his battered body. She would work on his mind next, he could tell, and, find a way, if she dared, to work on his troubled soul.

"I'm going to have to get you to a hospital, Lover Boy," Zouzou said, sponging down his torso with warm salt water. "You likely have broken ribs, ruptures, fractures. Your jaw looks broken."

He closed his puffy, half-shut eyes and gestured, "No."

"No? Are you kidding me? You need medical attention. You need help. I'll call Priscilla, and she can convince you for herself, and for the sake of your kids."

He took her wrists and applied pressure:

"No. Just leave me here."

"Why didn't you insist on getting the money? You damn well earned it."

"Blood money."

"Your blood."

"The price of my freedom."

Zouzou went out to buy bandages, gauze, and any painkillers she could purchase at the local drug store in the Village. She also needed provisions to make him something to eat and drink. While she was out, he raised himself up, rolled onto his bruised side, as best he could, used his arms to lift his body and shakily struggled to get to his feet. Lover Boy had to get back to work: to beg for help. Since he still needed cash, with not much hope of getting it on his own, he had to find someone who would give it to him, no questions asked. Stealing it or killing for it were not off the table yet, not much, but, given the way he felt, he opted for *beggin'* for it first.

3

City Life

Lover Boy was with Zouzou now in the apartment. She represented the urban life that he loved or thought he did with the identification of social stimulus, café life, theatres, galleries and so on. Zouzou looked strikingly beautiful in a simple outfit. She immediately sensed his anguish and hesitation.

"Do you want to make me cry, Lover Boy, and leave me for your wife?"

"I want to talk to you about everything, yes," he said, "and about *us*. I have to decide. We have to decide even when the choice is not clear or simple. I'm confused. I'm struggling. I want both. I feel trapped. I want you and the city, and yet I still want Priscilla, my children, and what that place has for us."

"You want both, but you won't commit to either of us," she said, touching his face, "and by doing so, you pin us down through your indecision."

"I'm walking around in a brain fog, lost in the Pandemic, feeling neither really alive, nor dead, but imagining I'm not."

"Dead?"

"Not alive."

With the mention of death on a day like this with its memorable blows, the *beggin'*, the stories, the clowning around, just to survive, he had to be resilient. He had to endure the blows to make it. Since superstitions died hard, especially when he was trying to figure out what to do and where to turn, the mention of death hit him hard. When would the moment come? Why be cruel to guys like Lover Boy?

"Let me make a decision," he thought.

What could possibly prevent it?

"It feels as if everything has been lost," he told Zouzou. "I feel that everything has gone away, and that nothing good has really stayed."

"Why can't you believe that it's just stored up, and that the past is

not over?" she said. "Nobody can undo what you've done. If you've suffered, and worked through your suffering, well, that stays with you. It
stays with all of us, even when you're not there."

Was that not part of Dr. Sparrow's approach to healing?

"It feels as if there is nothing inside," he said. "No motivation. No
energy. I feel an emptiness that is so deep and dark that it overwhelms
me. I'm imploding. What means anything anymore? How can I give
anything to anyone in the face of what is happening? How can I find
meaning in anything when I'm so scared, so overwhelmed, and so
tired?"

"Why do you have so much contempt for people?" Zouzou asked.
"Forgive their stupidity, their incompetence. Why not search for good-
ness? Is there jealousy and envy to the point of wanting to kill them?
Why not enjoy the beauty even of the smallest things: a sunset, a child?
Why let fear take over? What about wonder?"

"Because the vultures gloat," he said, "bloated on the carcasses of
success and failure, devouring everything and spitting out the losers,
the hungry and the poor."

Eventually, he worked it out with Zouzou that what was needed
was to get everyone together in one place and talk it over or figure it
out *together*, and find meaning in the ridiculous situation they were in.

"Won't Priscilla be hurt?"

"She's already hurting."

"You're going to get me to walk into her house, your lover? That's
crazy, Lover Boy. Why humiliate her? You'd make me go there? Maybe,
what you're looking for is here already."

"I've got to see you together. We can bring Joe Bucco with us. His
jokes might help to lessen the shock."

Was this his new scheme: to try to keep both women and both
places and have them agree to it? Or was it better to see them together
and make a choice on the spot by means of comparison? Heads or tails:
it was a gamble. What kind of decision was that? Was it a projected
experiment in living together? Was it a way of making the decision: to
choose by choosing each other, and to accept the fact that he couldn't
make a choice by himself, and that he had to have both? Maybe, just
maybe, in this city life, what he was looking for was already looking for
him. Off they went to see Priscilla and the girls. No joke.

4

Ana and Lina

Downstairs, the family dog, Weenie, was barking his doggy bobblehead off at Joe Bucco, but yielding and giving in to Zouzou's calculated caresses. Lover Boy was upstairs with Priscilla and the girls.

"You brought that woman into this house," Priscilla said, lifting the baby, Lina, out of her crib.

"She has a name," he said, holding their eldest daughter's (Ana's) hand.

"Of course, she has a name," Priscilla whispered close to her husband's face, "your *bitch*. And that strange man, ugly as a bug, a stranger, clowning around, a constant buffoon, you brought him here when I'm trying so hard to protect the girls from Covid."

"Do you want me to test them?"

"From what they're saying, they're Anti-Vaxxers, just back from Ottawa. I can just imagine what they picked up there, and what infections they're carrying around, and have brought into our place. Why are you demoralizing me more than you already do? What are you doing, Lover Boy?"

"I'm trying to figure everything out," he said, "not in isolation, or back and forth, but together at the same time and in same place. I think you'll learn to like Zouzou. As for Bucco, he's a clown with nothing but kindness in his big, fat, comic heart. We've got to work it out together."

He walked down with Ana. The little girl was nervous to meet the *guests*. Weenie was still trying to attack Bucco and kept barking and snarling at the jovial man until he mollified the dog by lobing bite-size chunks of cheese in the direction of Weenie's open mouth. Priscilla carried Lina in her arms in a tight embrace. Lover Boy put the dog outside to let her drop more turds in the snowbound backyard. The dog kept barking.

It wasn't long before the girls were entertaining, with songs and dances, the folks sitting in the living room. Lover Boy had made coffee, and Priscilla was serving it. Bucco was doing all the talking, trying to keep things light and moving. He improvised with exaggerated anecdotes and silly examples of self-deprecating humour. Zouzou was on the floor playing with the kids, saying how beautiful they were, how bright, how verbal, and how precious. They were talking up a storm with an eloquence beyond their years. While Priscilla hovered over them, staying nearby at all times, Lover Boy stood in the doorway.

"How can you not fall in love with these little beauties?" Zouzou asked. "You can talk to them about anything, and they understand it all."

The kids loved saying her name: "*Zouzou, Zouzou.*" Priscilla couldn't help liking someone that gushed over her girls. Despite her feelings of frustration and even betrayal, she felt stronger than Zouzou. If not superior to her, then more grounded. If less free, at least, more significant somehow. They began talking about little Lina's cute ways and beautiful Ana's many talents. The girls were showing Zouzou their dance moves, as well as pulling out all the toys and games they owned, and laying them at her feet.

"You're lucky," Zouzou said to Priscilla. "You have *them.*"

"You're luckier," Priscilla said. "You live in the city and get to do all the things I once loved to do."

"The city is not what it was," Zouzou said. "It feels more dangerous, and not much fun sometimes."

Bucco asked Lover Boy: "Why'd you bring us here, man? To see how you live when you live here? To get us to envy you?"

"Envy me?"

"You're a lucky man with a wife and kids, a house in a small town. Your kids seem so happy, but your wife, she is the saddest person I've ever seen, next to you."

When he looked over at his wife and his lover, Lover Boy noticed that they were getting along. Bucco pointed out how much they resembled one another. Zouzou was cuddling the baby, kissing her neck, smelling her skin, totally smitten by her beauty. At the same time, she was holding Ana's hand.

They had something to eat. Later, they listened to music, and played with the girls until bath time and the inevitable bedtime. Zouzou insisted that she wanted to help Priscilla bathe and settle the children.

Priscilla let her when the girls begged their mother to permit Zouzou to come upstairs with them. A giggle-fest ensued with splashing and plashing water and much screaming in sheer delight.

"Your wife wants what Zouzou has," Bucco said, "and your mistress wants what your wife has."

They spoke about how things seemed to come in twos: how people and situations doubled, or paired up, mirrored each other, and became their opposites. They talked about doubling, and then marrying opposites.

The women toweled off the gigglers. They dressed the girls in their pajamas, read them stories, one in one room, and the other in the other room, and then switched.

Later, the conversation was about the children with Zouzou doing most of the talking. With so much praise... was it believable? Was Zouzou planning something? Priscilla wanted to talk about other matters, but demurred. She didn't like conflict and confrontation. She would get up and leave, if ever she sensed tension.

Bucco said he would go out to buy provisions.

"It's only fair, and the least I could do."

Lover Boy went with him to pick up what they needed. When they got back, they put the groceries away. Bucco began preparing a late dinner. He was a great cook. Who knew? He said that he enjoyed preparing meals and liked sitting down to a good *feast*, as he said, with everyone sitting at the table together, and not just sitting around somewhere willy-nilly with plates teetering on their laps.

At the kitchen table, he launched into his views of the circumstances that they found ourselves in these days, and what could be done about it.

"The key is to come up with something creative and different," he said, "especially after the fear of the Pandemic, and the uncertainty of life itself. I mean, the deal is that everything comes in twos. Everything doubles as a double of itself: this/that, and here/there and /me/you and so on. It's a mirror with two images. You're the thing you look at most, if you stare at it hard enough. Somewhere in the world is your twin. There's a positive and negative of ourselves duplicated elsewhere."

Lover Boy saw his wife's spitting image, split in two, in the likeness of Zouzou. He was seeing things: seeing double, one woman the reflection of the other. He had slept with both.

"You're going crazy, Joe," Zouzou said. "Where is your double vision going to get us?"

"When you're here," Bucco said, "you want to be there. When you're there, you dream of being here. A double nostalgia effect. The same goes for people. You don't love the one you're with; you love the one you're not with. Back and forth, up and down, win or lose, but you're never with the one you want to be with."

He was hitting close to home, too close. Lover Boy gave him a warning look.

"All right, okay, but it's the same with where you're living, am I right? When you live here, you want to live elsewhere. When you're elsewhere, you want to be here. With jobs, too: you don't like what you're doing; you like what you're not doing. It's not your fault. You've got to dream it up and make it happen, or just let it happen."

"The whole thing is weird," Lover Boy said. "Best to tear it all down. Wait to see if it's worth starting over."

"Mere anarchy?" Zouzou said.

Priscilla looked frightened.

"Dreamed of in this lifetime," he said, quoting something he had once written based on something he had read or seen, "a new world, just beyond *now*."

"Man, you should've been some kind of poet," Bucco said. "Wild. But when you're not laughing at the world, you're crying for it."

"He used to write poetry," Priscilla said.

"Until I stopped," Lover Boy said.

"What stopped you?" Zouzou asked.

"I started quarreling with the *words*," he said. "You've got to ask them what to say, or they *ain't* talking, anymore. Not to you, anyway."

"Words fail, you mean," Bucco said. "I could've told you that."

"They don't fail," Lover Boy said. "You do. I failed them."

Bucco offered him a drink from a flask that he carried in his jacket pocket.

"Take a swig of that, and cheer up," he said. "It'll loosen your tongue and get you speaking poetry again. One thing is sure: this never fails."

He made a great late supper for them. It felt like family dinner. Priscilla said so. Lover Boy had failed in that department, too.

"I was thinking," Bucco said. "We could figure out a way of making cash, but never giving up the fun of working the way we want to."

"Such as making movies," Zouzou said.

"What kind of movies?" Lover Boy asked.

"Like the one I made in Ottawa that you two starred in," she said. She took out her smartphone.

"I'll show it to you, if you hook me up to the TV."

When they went into the living room, Lover Boy obliged her. They were soon watching footage from the Freedom Convoy and the Protest: trucks, protesters, cops, intimate shots of Lover Boy, and Bucco goofing around, or making a speech, and even Bob Lancaster appeared on the screen. Priscilla sat, looking frightened.

"It deserves an Academy Award," Bucco said. "Sell it and make a profit: a witness of the events. Your personal view is worth something, isn't it?"

"Exactly nothing," Lover Boy said.

"You're laughing at me," Bucco said, "laughing at all of us. Just wait until you have to laugh at yourself."

5

The Kidnapping

N o time to appraise the artistic merit of Zouzou's *film*: to give it a thumbs up or a thumbs down, or to create the laugh track that Lover Boy wanted to add to it. A horn with unrelenting violence blared on the street outside the rented house and got their shocked attention.

On high alert, Bucco went to the window, drew the curtain aside, and said, "Lancaster's rig."

"What's he doing here?" Zouzou broke out, likely knowing the answer.

"How did he find me?" Lover Boy had to know.

"His money, remember?" Bucco replied. "You can't cheat bastards like Bob without him avenging himself on the thief or thieves. Priscilla and Zouzou, go upstairs and look after the kids, and barricade yourselves. Lover Boy and I will have to deal with the vengeful jerk. So, while something is happening here, trying to get along, something is also going on out there, attempting to smash things apart. At the same time, it has to happen: not a coincidence, but a parallel occurrence. Everything comes in twos. Everything doubles."

"Yup, Bob Lancaster still hunting me down," Lover Boy said, "while I'm trying to figure things out."

"We got to stand up to him," Bucco said. "We have to take a stand. Otherwise, everything will be for nothing."

"This won't mean anything, if he gets his way, and wants to do us in."

"It'll mean what it means, but for now, *we* must stand up to him for *anything* to mean *anything* at all."

"What does it matter what he does? It just doesn't matter."

"It does matter. The women matter. Don't your kids matter? We've got to protect them if he tries anything. It matters if it comes to blows. Besides, you're responsible for them. What's the matter with you?"

"I can't even begin to tell you."

"*Che guaio*—I mean, we're facing some serious trouble. Wake up, man. We can't mess up, not with guys like Lancaster. No telling what he'll do, especially if he is packing."

"Nothing else matters now but to get him to stop blaring that horn."

"We gotta stop him."

"I'll go out."

"No, I'll see if I can talk to him first. Absorb the blow, if he wants to strike first. Don't come out, unless you have to."

"I don't want him in here."

"Nobody does. Just wait inside."

Bucco went out to deal with Lancaster. At the very least, he would try to get him to stop leaning on the horn. From the upstairs window, Priscilla and Zouzou saw Joe heading to the semi looming in front of the house, his arms outstretched, purposefully, but almost comically, like an amateur goalie trying to stop a professional hockey player's powerful slapshot.

"Who is he?" Priscilla wanted to know.

"A nasty piece of work," Zouzou said. "Nobody to mess with."

"Did my husband mess with him?"

"He did. It was a real mess. A bloody mess. Lover Boy stepped into it all right."

Lancaster got out of the truck and confronted Bucco. He ignored his jokey greeting and pushed him to the ground. Out of the trailer, two men emerged, kicked and punched Bucco. And then ran to the back of the house. Lover Boy was set to run outside to help the fallen man when he heard the intruders smash the back window and crash through the back door. Weenie was barking and threatening them. They had guns and were on the point of shooting the animal when Lover Boy charged them. Shots were fired. One of the two rushed upstairs, shouting Zouzou's name. The woman standing in front of him said: "It's me."

Since she said so, he attacked her and dragged her downstairs. No one could stop him. It was pointless to try to defend yourself. Who could against such blunt force and sudden brutality? She was dragged down the stairs and out the front door. The intruder shot Lover Boy in the leg. He couldn't pursue him. They took one of the women to the truck, and shoved her into the trailer, climbed in after her, and shut the door. Lancaster, who had been working Bucco over during the assault on the house, now jumped into the cab, put the rig into gear and got the hell out of there. Bucco's body lay unconscious on the boulevard.

Priscilla or someone looking like Priscilla ran downstairs to see Lover Boy struggling to get up. In his pain and panic, he thought it was his wife.

"See to Joe," he said. "See to Joe."

Lover Boy was wrapping his leg with a dish towel and willing himself to move into the living room. The barking dog woke the girls, never mind the crashing noise of the break-in and the gunshots. The baby was crying. The older child was screaming.

"I'm Zouzou," she said. "They took *her*, Lover Boy, Priscilla, not *me*, mistaking her for me. There's a likeness, right. We're dead ringers. She stepped out to confront them, no doubt wanting to make sure the girls were safe, prepared to die for them, and protecting me."

"They kidnapped my wife," he said.

"I'll call the police. I'll call for an ambulance. You're bleeding."

"No police. No ambulance. They'll kill her for sure. See to Bucco."

"You've been shot, Lover Boy. You need help."

"See to him."

"Ana and Lina are so upset."

"All right, go upstairs. Do what you can to settle them. Go on."

He tied a dishcloth around his leg as tightly as he could. Then stumbled down the hall, clinging to the walls, and went out to see what he could do for Bucco. When he bent over him and called his name, Bucco raised his arms, opened his eyes, and got up, as if out of a shallow grave.

"They took Priscilla," Lover Boy said.

"I told you she looked like Zouzou," Bucco said. "Lancaster wanted her."

"They hurt the dog."

"And you. They shot you."

"It's a massacre," Lover Boy said, helping Bucco back into the rented house.

"A kidnapping," Bucco said. "They kidnapped Priscilla."

6

Rescue Attempt

Bucco knew what to do, or believed he did, beyond bluffing. He tended to the dog, and patched her up. Then took care of Lover Boy. The bullet had gone through his right calf and now lodged in the kitchen floor. Lover Boy said that they had to get the girls out of there in case Lancaster returned once he saw the mistake that his skink-faced goons had made in the wrongful kidnapping. No knowing what he would do to Priscilla. Collateral damage. A way of punishing Lover Boy in taking his sweet revenge.

"Let's head back to the Big City," Bucco said. "We'll keep the girls safe in your apartment."

"Can you and Zouzou do that for me? Don't forget the dog. I want to stay here. Lancaster will be back. I want to deal with him if he tries again."

"What are you going to do next?"

"Clean up the mess."

"And then?"

"And then, I'm going to see a guy named Morphy."

Zouzou was amazing in her ability to comfort Ana and Lina. She got them dressed, prepared food and snacks, got together books and toys, packed everything up, and set off with Bucco and the dog to try to keep the children safe, away from the crime scene. She would do her best to be a good surrogate mother to them, a mother she resembled in more ways than her looks.

Lover Boy cleaned up the blood. Locked up and went out to see Morphy.

The stairs gave him a lot of trouble this time because of his wounded leg. The four flights were steep, but seemed steeper with a bad limp. He used an umbrella as a makeshift cane and made it to the top in pain.

"Morphy?"

"Back again? For more? This time, I'll kick the shit out of you. You stole my gun."

"Do you have *another*?"

"What did you do with the gun?"

"Shot up the bags and threw the weapon into the creek. So, I need another gun."

"I got another gun. What kind of trouble are you in?"

"A guy named Lancaster has kidnapped my wife."

"Who is this Lancaster?"

"Bob Lancaster."

"The trucker?"

"That's the son-of-a-bitch."

"Son-of-a-bitch and bastard," Morphy said. "You involved with that psycho? Is it about money or a woman?"

"Both."

"You need more than a gun."

"What do I need?"

"*Me*. You need Morphy."

"That's you. Do I need you?"

"Hell, yes. If everyone were like me, we'd have a better world."

"You'll help me?"

"Better than killing you. Do I have to punch you in the face again?"

"If you want."

"I'll kick your ass later," Morphy said. "Save my energy for tracking down Lancaster. I still owe him for what he did to my business dealings, the cheat, the bandit. Let's go."

"I don't have a vehicle."

"Or a gun. Not to worry. I've got both, and plenty of ammo, and contacts. I'll make some calls. Then off we go. We're always on our guard for things to happen, especially violent situations, always looking over our shoulders, but we need something special as in this case."

"What do we need?"

"Firepower."

Morphy did what he said he was going to do. Once in the Jeep, Lover Boy filled Morphy in on what had happened in Ottawa, and what had gone down at the rented house.

"He's got your woman," Morphy said. "We'll get her back. Just as long as you do exactly as I say. Don't contradict me. Just watch."

Morphy was killing himself laughing. He was laughing in anticipation of what he was going to do to Lancaster once he got hold of him.

He made a call to an associate of his named Laffigan. Laffigan told him he was *on it*.

"They're going to ransack his house until we get there," Morphy said, "and take anything of value and then destroy the place. Lancaster will find it in ruins when he arrives."

"What if he goes somewhere else?"

"He'll hear about the destruction and react. Guys like him don't think. They just react. Impulse. No brains. You can't touch anything belonging to him without him shitting himself and then hitting out beyond all proportion. But we'll hit him first and harder."

"My wife?"

"This Morphy you're riding with has a chivalrous side."

"What?"

"Rescue. We're going to rescue your woman, because she's a woman. I know that women don't want to be rescued these days, but I want to do it in honour of the way things used to be. I'm also big on revenge."

"You're a funny guy, Morphy."

"You're a sad man, a sad-sack. Cheer the hell up, despite the limp. I'll get you a proper cane, and you can get rid of that umbrella. You're riding with Morphy now. Your enemy happens to be my enemy. Maybe, one day you'll have my back. This is a happy day for you. Getting your wife back may turn out to be the best day of your life so far."

7

Playing Family

Morphy drove them to a place in the north end of the city. His men, in pick-up trucks, at Laffigan's instigation, were already driving across Bob Lancaster's front lawn, as if in demolition or stock car racing. One of the trucks had several lengths of chain hitched to the back and attached to Lancaster's front porch, in a tug of war, aggressively pulling down the columns. The driver revved his engine and drove away as fast as he could from the property. The porch collapsed. Morphy liked seeing it fall.

"Are you getting excited, Cade? Are we having fun yet?"

"Excited? Fun? Not exactly."

"Revenge is exciting. Both striking *first* and striking *fast* in getting the better of Lancaster lead to the kind of *fun* I'm talking about."

True enough: the speed of violence and the swiftness of revenge were dizzying on this scale. On the inside, under Laffigan's direction, Morphy's men invaded Lancaster's house with crowbars and long-handled axes, hacking away at the cluttered interior. They were after complete destruction, as ordered and ordained by Morphy himself. Laffigan found Lancaster's safe, and with the aid of other destructors, hauled it out of the house for safekeeping, and as a means of bargaining for Priscilla's release. The exchange would consist of the safe for the safety of the woman. This was the kind of violence that Lover Boy hadn't imagined possible, despite his need to be punished by being punched in the face, and bringing everything down in an anarchic power play. This was a demolition crew that destroyed your enemy's defenses in a sneak attack before the enemy could destroy yours.

Morphy counted on somebody getting in touch with Lancaster and filling him in on what was going on at his place. That was Laffigan's job. He did it with zeal, and embellished the communication as much as his dark imagination would allow. He was a wickedly imaginative agent. Having done what they wanted to do, and having taken what they had been told to take, Morphy's men cleared off to wait for the showdown, the throwdown, the confrontation. They did not run away and hide. Rather, they had even raided Lancaster's refrigerator and bar and had helped themselves to what refreshments they required after the exhaustion of their demolition work. In the aftermath of the hard work they had done, Morphy and Lover Boy now sat waiting just down the road from Lancaster's destroyed house.

"Sit tight," Morphy said. "Won't be long. Won't be long now. News travels fast on the revenge hotline, thanks to my man, Laffigan, when yours truly and his people get through with your property and assets. In this case, Lancaster's."

Within the next hour, Lancaster drove his semi down the street and parked it in front of the shambles of his ruined home. His men jumped out of the truck. Where was Priscilla?

"She's likely bound and gagged in the trailer," Morphy said. "I'll take care of Lancaster. You get to save her. It calls for heroics, even with a wounded leg. I'll take care of the firepower."

An ambush. Morphy's men *took care* of Lancaster's operatives and henchmen. Morphy then bargained with Lover Boy's enemy, his too. What else could Lancaster do but give Morphy want he wanted? He would live to kill him another day, but get back his safe today. The safe on the back of a pick-up truck was dumped onto the front lawn amid all the other debris.

Lover Boy opened the trailer to find Priscilla tied up and secured in the back. Freed her. Held her. Helped her down and then led her to Morphy's waiting car.

"Where to?" Morphy wanted to know.

"Downtown," Lover Boy said.

"Why there?" Priscilla asked.

"That's where the kids are," he said, and then spoke to Morphy. "I owe you, Morphy. I don't know what I would have done to get her back without you."

"You would have got her," Morphy said, "if you were *Morphy*."

"I'm not."

"No, you're not Morphy. I am."

"You helped me, despite what previously went down between us."

"Better than a kick in the ass."

"Or a punch in the face."

"Now get your shit together, Cade. Stop thinking the way you do.

Think like *me*. Think like Morphy. In future, be more Morphy-like."

Before they left the scene, Laffigan approached Lover Boy.

"By the way," he said, "I was the guy that called you to clean up the dogshit. I thought I could get to Morphy's place in time, but I was too late."

He wanted to pay Lover Boy for his work and for all the misunderstanding.

"Morphy paid it in full," Lover Boy said, "and so did you. Without the misunderstanding, we never would have met."

Laffigan laughed and signalled his goodbye. Morphy drove Lover Boy and Priscilla to the apartment and left them to figure out the rest of their lives. Was this what was supposed to happen? Lover Boy and Priscilla found the kids playing with Zouzou and Bucco on the living room floor of the mostly bare apartment. They were playing a game called "Family" that involved a reversal of roles with the kids playing the parents and the adults playing the children. When Ana and Lina saw their mother, they ran to her. She knelt down and embraced them both.

"Don't cry, Mummy. Don't cry."

"You have beautiful children," Zouzou said.

She was just about to say that she wanted what the other woman had, but refrained from saying it once she caught sight of Lover Boy's undeniably sad and imploring eyes.

Bucco, despite his injuries, put on a wonderful spread from the provisions that he had procured. They had what the girls called an indoor picnic with a blanket spread out on the floor in continuation of the game they called *Family*. The little ones were thrilled, serving as best they could what was laid out in front of them.

After the *picnic*, Priscilla and Zouzou took the kids into the bathroom to wash up and prepare for bed. The little girls wanted to sleep in the living room, now cleared of plates and food trays. The eldest fell asleep in Zouzou's arms, while the youngest fell asleep in the maternal grip and clasp of her mother's sobbing embrace.

Lover Boy and Bucco went out onto the balcony and talked over what had happened, and what to do next.

"I've got to get closer to a decision," Lover Boy said. "But I have to find work."

"Finding work is my speciality, remember," Bucco said. "Creative, not soul-destroying work. I've got some ideas. See if you like them."

"What are they?"

"No, no, you have to see what I'm suggesting while on the job, not in your mind's eye. We'll start tomorrow. For now, I've got to change my bandages. How's your leg?"

"I haven't looked, but it's still throbbing."

"From the gunshot wound. You've got to have it looked at."

"They'll ask how I got it. Best to see how it goes, for good or ill. Less of a story to tell or of a gunfight to have to confess to."

"If questioned about it, say it was a stray bullet, wrong place at the wrong time, in a street shootout between rival gangs, or a drive-by shooting, common enough these days. You'd better let me take a look at the wound. Clean it out. Get goop and hydrogen peroxide to disinfect it."

"Better you than the cops."

"Better me than the embalmer and undertaker, if your wound doesn't heal."

They went in and found places to lie down. The living room resembled an encampment (only inside), such as any number of encampments that were springing up outside, in the ravine, not far from the apartment building. They had brought the outside inside, and taken the inside out, just as Florinda or any nature-lover liked to do.

"We're the lucky ones," Bucco said.

"Lucky? How?"

They were lucky, if surviving Lancaster's assault were deemed lucky, and lucky if to have the children sleeping in the arms of two beautiful women were also considered *lucky*. Weren't they lucky to have someone patch up their wounds? What about the luck of knowing someone as vengeful as Morphy, and of having him on your side? So, they agreed, switching to a laughing mood, that they were lucky, the luckiest luckless losers in the world.

8

Jobs

Bucco gushed and then overflowed with ideas and schemes for making money.

"'No work is beneath us,' my mamma used to say, working like hell her whole life long."

Even though he was likely talking about the dignity of work, he claimed that he was interested in original and meaningful ways of earning a living.

"What about billboards?" Bucco asked.

"What about them?"

"You know: installing them," he said. "What about fallers: cutting down trees? Or being undertakers? Earth blasters? Underwater demolition divers? Dinky Operators, moving rocks and stuff. Escalator Installers? Selling Ice Cream?"

"You're going wild again, Bucco."

"The wilder, the better. The better, the freer you feel. Cade, you know what your problem is?"

"Yes, I walk with a limp and a cane that Morphy gave me."

"Besides that. You've got a limp brain. Nothing means anything to you. So, you use that as an excuse to do nothing."

"Ice cream? Scooping it, you mean?"

"Getting to know all about it, the history of it, for example, and how my people, the Sicilians, say, invented it, making it, selling it in an interesting way. Look, what I'm saying is that you've got to dig deep into yourself to figure out what gets you excited. Do what you *feel*. Picture it, man, and steer right for it. Not in yourself or in the dark, but beyond yourself, and outside of here."

He pointed to Lover Boy's head.

"Way out there, and up there. Picture tomorrow and make it happen."

"Look, Bucco, I've had a lot of jobs. Done a lot of things to pay the bills."

"Like what?"

"Worked on the roads. Worked as a roofer. Played in a band."

"Music?"

"Music, what else? Guitarist for a band called *Mamalujo*. Taught music, too. Worked in a movie house. Had a factory job. Mucked out stables. I was even a barber for a while. And a farmhand. Worked in a grocery store. Did electrical work. Construction. Delivered groceries. Pruned trees. Sold Used Cars. Did maintenance in an old folk's home. Bartended. Cleaned up dog shit. Name it, Bucco, I likely did it. Couldn't keep it steady, though. Part-time jobs always, or on contract. Nothing that would give me work until I retire, as it used to be."

"Those days are gone. These days, you got to do several things at once. Moonlighting is the only way."

"And that's supposed to give you a meaningful work experience? A permanent part-timer?"

"I'm saying go crazy, doing something wild."

"I could learn all about ice cream, scoop it, serve it, lick it off my fingers, play in a band, work in a factory, cut down trees, muck out stables, deliver groceries, do maintenance, and so on, all at the same time; work 24 hours a day, and what would I have to show for the moonlighting at the end of it? *Nothing*. Just fatigue. Feeling defeated. Crushed. No security. No benefits. No future."

"You want to know how it will all turn out."

"Right."

"It will turn out the way you want it to, if it means something to you."

"But never the way it is supposed to, with dignity or without."

"Sounds like a religious thing with you."

"No, it's too late in the day to be a monk, mostly for sexual reasons, and the kids. Besides, if you set out to get rid of poverty, you're bound to fail, don't you, like all religious fools? Isn't that funny?"

"Not sure, funny-man. At least, not on your own," Bucco said, as if it were the punchline of an old joke.

9

Thanks for Nothing

"*Thanks for nothing,*" Lover Boy said, "*if the joke is on me.*"

They were tripping in Yorkville, a hair's breadth away from dropping the whole project. His body sagged. He limped, head hanging down, staring at his feet. Bucco leaned in close. It was always too close for Lover Boy's comfort being next to him. Forced to listen to Bucco's *speechifying*, he had to endure it, as he shot his mouth off, triggering resentment.

"Poverty, as a kind of beauty, is a whole other thing."

He was also asking Lover Boy, just asking:

"Are the poor *poor*, or do we make them poor?"

Lover Boy snuffled. Shrugged it off. Then whispered without looking at him:

"As ever, Bucco, you're not thinking straight. You're just talking."

He had other uses for beauty. He brooded on the past with its beautiful yet lost consolation prizes.

"Poverty always costs money," he broke out. "Think of the money, man. Making it is one thing, but keeping it is still another. Money is the point on this planet."

Bucco needed to know why, saying what he really couldn't say, but he gave it to Lover Boy full in the face:

"Is money the living end? Is it the effing goal. Is the money-ball the be-all and end-all?"

"Money is money," Lover Boy said, "and money is *never* mine. What else do you want me to say, Bucco? And where are you going with this? Where are we going?"

"You'll find out soon enough."

"I want it all," Lover Boy rapped to the bass of his own beat-box heart, "but if I have to make money off of beauty, this wannabe rich man *wants* to leave feeling homeless behind. If and when that happens, I'll keep you posted."

Was he talking to his own mouth? Or was Bucco getting to him?

"I get it," he said.

"What? What do you get?"

"Broken dreams, man, lives strewn on the streets. Now, shut the hell up, you anarchist."

"I can give these broken dreamers my thoughts about failure."

"What's that?"

"Not that I failed," Lover Boy said, "but that I lost my deal with reality, and my ideals."

"Now, you're talking," Bucco said, hearing only the last half of his sentence.

"But outside any hostel," Lover Boy blatted, "it's always winter, spring, summer, and fall. So, honour our downfall with life's regrets and missteps."

"Welcome to the way it is," Bucco breathed back. "Get real. We're here."

"Where?"

Bucco had taken him to a barber shop for a hipster haircut.

"You need a new look," Bucco went on, "or a flashback in a mixture of wine or beer or platinum, if you recollect the fifties, and look good in black."

"Who doesn't?" Lover Boy asked.

"Get a manicure," Bucco yawped, leading him into the shop, "for your down-and-out nails. Get the perfect haircut, if you're worthy of your wounds with matted or even unruly hair. And if you're shocked by neglect and fear of open spaces, struck twice by lightning, the barber will try to tame your capillary clots and knots, blood curls and whorls with a high, tight fade."

Bucco greeted the barber and motioned for him to take his friend first. Lover Boy swung his bad leg up and sat in the chair.

"You're telling yourself a story," he said, "but you're just singing Figaro."

The barber talked to him about the cut.

"With a little effort, I can get you to look more like Elvis than you already do."

"Do your dirty work," Lover Boy said. "I'm leaving it up to you. Just tell me what you're doing while you're doing it."

"I'll narrate trimming the sideburns and touching up the quiff," the barber said, "as I explain to you what I'm doing and take the pearl-handled straight razor to the chin just as I do to any gender. I'll even do the scabbed-over eyebrows. Then cut and snip hair off the top to reveal a 1950's head, and make your green, brown, blue or gold eyes pop. For bloodshot eyes, I'll tint the hair black, or restore the coils of your dying head snakes. To cover scars especially on damaged cheeks, I'll give you the sheen and lustre of orang-utans; or I'll tonsure your hair if you're playing chess with St. Francis' beloved and homeless poor in Moss Park. This hipster barber will wash, blow-dry, cut, comb, and style an ex-con's hair, *pro bono*, just as I cut my own."

"I don't live on the street yet," Lover Boy said, "but I do have a police record."

"I'm just playing with you," the barber said. "It's all for free."

"You can't do it for *free*, not for long," Lover Boy corrected him. "Man, it's just a long suicide for all of us, if everything were for free."

"For free," the barber said, working on Lover Boy's head, "because freedom is something for nothing. No *quid pro quo* or *tit for tat*. Forty hours a week, getting behind my dummy when I was at beauty school and dreaming of making cash hand over fist with big tips from filthy rich clients, I know, but now I want to set up a retro barbershop, or just work out there after dark in the long-haired park."

"There's a hidden grievance in everything you're telling me," Lover Boy said. "You'll go hungry."

"So, I'll go hungry, and I'll stay hungry," the barber said, jumped-up.

"But you needed to be certified to be a barber, like any angel-head-ed Victor or Sam with shocks of white hair, or any barber surgeon, like Figaro, for the sake of the barber pole. You've got to recover your losses."

"Yeah, and I wanted to stay hungry and stay foolish, working on anybody's hair in the streets, like a renegade monk wielding a pearl-handled straight razor instead of a cross with rosary beads, and doling out coffee and coins and free haircuts, occasionally digging into the beggars' banquet with those *beggin'* at their own doors by giving them unclaimed tips from the tip jar, the spare change I'll make from oc-casionally doing rich mannequin heads. Being drawn to something doesn't make it real. Doing what you dream *does*. You're not a lover just because you talk about love day and night. You're a lover when you love with mind, body and soul. What virtue are you drawn to: cour-age, kindness, compassion?"

"Where are you going with this, man?" Lover Boy wanted to know why the barber was leaving barbering before making his fortune. He had no interest in his notion of virtue. He was likely talking about talent.

"I'm leaving my dummy behind," the barber said. "I'm leaving the Yorkville salon, right at the beginning of fingering and clasping hair-raising dollar bills."

"Just to *feel* free," Lover Boy said.

"Saying the words, *for free*," the barber whispered, "is a freedom song sung for nothing outside a barbershop."

With what he was after, in the brave, new dream he was chasing down, after quitting the making of money, he figured he'd get to know hundreds and hundreds of hairs on the heads of hundreds and hundreds of needy heads.

When he was done with Lover Boy, Bucco sat in the barber chair and got a haircut. He was on speaking terms with the barber, Phil. Soon enough, after paying and tipping the barber, Lover Boy and Bucco were both out of the shop, saying:

"He made us pay, despite all that talk. Thanks for nothing."

Amidst the noise of the city, Lover Boy was out of there, not a moment too soon. The talk was driving him crazy. His hobbling feet landed on the street with a bad limp. Bucco said he looked like Elvis Presley on a stamp with a great haircut. Talk carried them along to Bloor and Bay. According to Bucco, they were on the cusp of meeting somebody named "Poor Excuse," and Lover Boy knew him from school days gone by. The hook-up was for a flick. They met and greeted, and took the escalator up to the Varsity Cinema. Poor Excuse wouldn't pay, because he couldn't, and so Bucco dug into his shirt pocket and pulled out the necessary bills for three tickets. It didn't matter what movie they were seeing, did it? This was a chance to meet somebody that could give them a lead on a great job, if maybe a little on the shady side of the street. It was just a kind of homage to what they used to do way back when before *making it* wasn't even in their vocabulary. True, they didn't give a shit then. Was *now* the same as *then*, or just a shout-out to old times? Thanks for nothing to those who think they know, but would soon find out. *Laugh here.*

10

Foreign Versus Domestic Films

As if passing Lover Boy along, Bucco re-introduced him to their criminal friend, the guy he claimed he had nicknamed Poor Excuse.

"Advance notice," Poor Excuse was saying, "because, in the opening scene, she's sitting at the kitchen table quietly crying for no good reason that you can see. A loaded handgun spins on the tabletop, and so you ask her what the matter is, and sip your black coffee; and she says she's just sitting there, eyes half shut, and that nothing is the matter. A cup of coffee rests like a tiny, perfect bomb in front of her in the ceremonial refusal to talk to you. She's enclosed, secretive. You let the ticking of the kitchen clock take the place of words. *Despair* is a word, and so is *grief.* Take your pick of bitterness, resentment. And, as the leading man checks the time, it's over and done with. She says: 'I don't want to see you anymore.'"

The freak wasn't talking about the film they were going to see, but about what had happened back there in his recent past: the mess he had made and left behind, or some mess he was on the point of making in the near future. To Lover Boy, the last line sounded vaguely familiar from his own past.

"Spoiler alert," Poor Excuse said, "because it's not happening, not in this lifetime, not in this movie, and it's not how things are going to turn out in this reel, directed by me, and starring yours truly."

He said it that way for old time's sake, but Poor Excuse also threw down with:

"And where are you off to, lover? Isn't that what you said? The credits aren't rolling by yet to end the flick."

He wouldn't stand for his own blather, or anybody else's. It wasn't the same today as it was yesterday. It was ever the way it was, or maybe it wasn't. But Bucco said he preferred foreign films to domestic. Poor Excuse slapped him hard on the back of the head, and declared:

"Nothing is for free in either a foreign or domestic life, or the next."

Since it was *Peekaboo Thursday*, as he called it, they were watching the watchers in the movie house with Poor Excuse set to jump the gangland guy and his girl in the fifth row, and then shifted eyes back to the black and white screen, the male gaze now gazing at the other guy's male gaze. The weird guy was saying:

"Every mess gets cleaned up eventually."

He got it in first and uttered his words in the dark:

"I'm like the guy from public works who cleans up road kills. You never see me. I just do it, or the good soldier who deals with the aftermath of war. Everything gets cleaned up. In the promise of the future, you double-booked the past, and I had to deal with your disinterest when I said it wouldn't last. 'Do something about the mess,' you said. Then shat the bed hard."

Leaning forward, standing up, Poor Excuse grabbed Bucco by the arm and said:

"I got *this*."

He was already up, and in the aisle, heading to the fifth row. Lover Boy and Bucco were treated to a foreign film about a domestic dispute, R-rated and with live action. Violent. A guy, nicknamed No Chance, a guy Lover Boy knew and a guy that knew both Zouzou and him personally, was taken a beating at the hands of Poor Excuse, deserved or undeserved, in front of his girl.

"I'm sick of jealous rivals," the victim said, missing a tooth or two.

"I'm sick of crumb-throwing flirts," Poor Excuse said, wailing away with bloody fists.

Poor Excuse contended that she was a flirt, a sweet cheat, and that her temporary date was a thief who had stolen her from him. They were both disposable, as far as he could tell. He'd crawl on his belly to slime them both. To Lover Boy's way of thinking, Poor Excuse was just cleaning up the mess that the cheater had made, and leaving his own mess crying and bleeding in the seat. Now, their goal was to get out of there fast, and, fast and faster, Poor Excuse, Bucco and Lover Boy tripped up the aisle and down the escalator, and that was what they did, with him, the slowpoke, Jack (Lover Boy) Cade, grimacing, limping and lagging behind the slime. *Laugh track. Cut.*

11

Tagging the Walls

Poor Excuse was leading the charge, getting the hell out of there, and out onto the street. He was killing himself laughing. At least, that was like old times, the way it was. So was the take on violent action, not just for kicks in chick flicks.

"It's a pornographic age," he said as they headed off to a nearby café.

"Are you still watching porn, you *Poor Excuse* for a human being, or making it, or both?" Bucco chafed him.

"Who isn't? But I'm talking about the powers-that-be. I remember when the Americans elected a Porn President, and will again, and it set off an age of conspiracies and deceit."

"Because he had paid for sex with a porn star?"

"That, and his need for fascist power that messes with people, and sucks the brains out of his followers. He wanted to build walls, and we want to tear them down. That is, some of us."

"Who?"

"Those of us that I want you to join to keep that sort of thing from happening here. You'll get well paid for it."

Then they saw a graffiti girl tagging a wall. Poor Excuse knew her or thought he did or wanted to. He got out of her that her name was June. She was spraying her claims on back-alley walls, in protest against the urban sprawl. She tagged her street name, *Juno*, as a moniker, taken from the Greek goddess of marriage, the jilted and wronged Queen of the ancient world.

"She was beautiful once before *god* raped her in the woods with the gift of a cuckoo bird."

June was reclaiming the one-time innocence of her neighbourhood. This graffiti artist did her *brain-dance* on bricks. To some, it was rude and crude, a disgrace to deface the architecture that they so loved: banks, shops, business backlots, signage that promised sweet deals for a steal. But with a feel for the real, this girl with a moustache didn't feel the same. No shame, no pain, no harm or blame as she carried her spray cans with pride, and advertised, as a poet once wrote of her, "a brave new phallus on an underwear ad, a paint-blackened tooth on the candidate's mouth, already re-elected."[5]

"So *blessed be* the graffiti artist," she said, "and her can of *quick dry* paint. Blessed be the vandal and her handle. Let there always be tribal alleyways for me to spray, and many different ways of denouncing the modern world, like primitive markings inscribed on cave walls."

"With that," Poor Excuse said, "I'm head over heels in love with her: June."

He left her to it: the first phase of what he called *the seduction in plain sight of the graffiti chick*. He stayed close, leaning against the wall, not daring to catch her eye at first, because you never know, and just watched her tagging the wall.

"Your friend took off fast," she said.

"He had to get going," Bucco said. "Going *nowhere* fast."

"Giddy-up," she said. "But you're still here."

"Interested in your work," he said.

"Not me?"

"Interested in *you*, too."

"Then carry my cans."

"I'll be back," Bucco said. "No time just now for the dance. I've got to get my unsettled pal settled first. Still, I'll be sure to look you up in the alleyway, looking for your tag, if I ever come back this way again."

---

5   Based on "Tagging the Walls" by Nic Labriola.

12

Cold Readings

Lover Boy realized how his story was being told, all the loves and the works of Jack Cade (a.ka. Lover Boy), as if contained in a headshrinker's dossier. What was in Dr. Sparrow's file on him? Maybe, his case was a detective's cold case. The truth was in the file folder. The folder contained a *beggin'* letter, copies of emails, cellphone records, excerpts from a fragmented memoir, fights, a kidnapping, messing around with ideas, and so on. It was based on shame and shaming, as if read aloud in a cold reading. Such a reading was a pastiche of borrowings: sayings that said too little or too much, but always about the self, himself, *himself.* Was he worthy of their wisdom? Reading the contents of the folder of himself was guesswork. He wanted to destroy it and begin again.

After, in considering what the hell had happened, and who the freaks were that Bucco had introduced him to, he said:

"Why did you take me to that subversive barber?"

"What about Poor Excuse?" Bucco was curious.

"Him, too, but first the barber," Lover Boy said. "I keep thinking about *him.*"

"Not the graffiti artist?"

"Her, too, by why the barber?"

"To get a radical haircut," Bucco said, "and an earful of the type of subversive tripe and socialist talk that has landed you in the shit repeatedly. Disaffection, anger, and resentment. He's throwing everything over for his project: to work for the homeless and make them look beautiful and all they can be."

"I hope he succeeds. And Poor Excuse guy, what was that about?"

"Crime as a career," Bucco said. "Weirdness as a way of living. I wanted you to see it for yourself and what it is, in case you're tempted. Violence is the currency. Money is his poor excuse for living. Payback and revenge are everything to him, like your man, Morphy."

"And the girl in the alley?"

"A political path, and using your talents to carve it out," Bucco said. "What about following her?"

"No thanks," Lover Boy said. "It's hard enough already, trying to figure things out without spraying walls. My struggle leads elsewhere."

"But for you, why not endure it?" Bucco said. "Shoulder it. Take a stand against what hurts you. Don't give in. Don't give up. There's something waiting for you, Cade. Do it."

"What do you want me to do? What's waiting for me?"

"How the hell should I know? Or anybody else. Search for it and find it."

"We have to get back," Lover Boy said. "I'll search for it and find it tomorrow."

Once back, lying on the floor in the apartment, next to the women, he didn't know why but he kept thinking about his grandmother. He was that far gone. How he'd seen her at the end of her life, asking if anyone could help her with her last breath, and lifting herself up, and, when she was told that nobody could come to her aid, only what and who she believed in, she had said:

"Then it's finished."

And she breathed her last. What did she believe at that moment? That though she was on the point of death, nobody could take from her the things that she had done and the places where she had been, and the suffering that she had endured, and the work that she had finished, and the people that she had loved. That was her completed masterpiece. No finishing touches needed. Her purpose was her work, and her love was the meaning of her life. All these things were now safely stored in the past. Her love and work were finished. Yes, no more *beggin'* for anything.

Why was he thinking about her, dead tired from the day, and unsure of what the next day would bring? Was this what was waiting for him? All that was left to do was laugh his head off or bawl his eyes out.

He was told afterward in the aftermath, coming out as dirty laundry, even though he could have figured it out for himself, that Priscilla and Zouzou were talking, taking the dirty laundry down to the laundry room in the basement, while he and Bucco looked after the kids.

"Lover Boy has changed so much," Priscilla said.

"The word *changed* doesn't begin to describe how much he's changed," Zouzou said. "I've seen it, too. Maybe, he's just revealing himself, declaring who he really is. Remember what he's been through."

"I don't know what can be done for him," Priscilla said. "What can I do? I don't know why he's so paralyzed by having to make decisions."

"He still loves us both, doesn't he?"

"Does he? Does he really care for me? Tell me. You tell me."

"He's become so inward, so lost in himself, fighting a personal battle."

"We never used to fight, and now it seems like a constant stand-off. All that is missing are the guns. We're both carrying wounds."

"You're paying a price, Priscilla. He's got to keep his ideals no matter what, and that is costly."

"He can keep whatever he wants, but what does he want?"

"To please you."

"By hurting me?"

"It hurts him, too."

"So many memories come back, no matter where I am, or what I'm doing, even laundry. I just break down."

"I'll talk to him," Zouzou promised, loading coins into the washing machine.

She was as good as her word once she went back upstairs.

"Lover Boy, let's talk. Joe, give us a few minutes."

He took the girls into the other bedroom to continue the game they were playing.

"You talk," he said. "I'll listen."

Zouzou laid it out for him as she saw it in her own Zouzouzian way: how vague he was, a repeat of Florinda's thoughts about him, how muddled, how contradictory (Dr. Sparrow's conception), and how hurtful (his mother's complaint). How critical he was of anyone with money (Spinski's view). How angry he got towards his creditors. How vicious he had become each time that he was forced to outface ignorant and stupid people. It seemed that they couldn't talk, and couldn't think, and couldn't act without making him furious, even vicious. Why didn't he just find it *funny and laugh it off*? How the Pandemic had left him feeling cheated and empty.

Zouzou said she knew how hard it was for him to think about the future. How would everything turn out? Who knew? Who understood what challenges tomorrow would bring? How could he face the responsibility of family, especially with little children? Why did he feel empty? What was he searching for? What was his crisis? What was un-

der it all? What could they do to help him? What was good enough for
him to go on with? Wasn't love enough? Why wasn't love the motivator,
or the connector? He needed to make sense of everything. But why
sink? Why not rise? What was the best thing to do? The status quo? Or
a complete overhaul of reality?

"The more you search for something, the farther away it gets from
you," he said. "The harder you fight, the greater are your losses."

"Don't fight us," Zouzou said. "Don't search for us. We're here,
Lover Boy, but not defenseless. Don't forget to choose *us*. Make a fresh
start."

He said that he'd heard it all before. Was making a fresh start a de-
nial of what had happened: the ones that had hurt him, and the ones
that he'd hurt, and what about those that were beyond reach, never to
be blamed? He never looked to get his own back. He did not avenge
himself, or look for revenge. Maybe, he should have. There was no fight
in him anymore, was there? Hadn't he stopped searching long ago?

"You let the propaganda get to you, Lover Boy," she said.

"I let the bastards win," he said. "So what? You can't even go for
a walk in the evening without hearing two old women yelling about
the government with *eff* this and *eff* that, *and* eff you-know-who. The
whole situation makes you eat your heart out. Is it really living, all this
beggin' for something you can't ever have?"

"Lover Boy, don't you want to live anymore?"

"Live?"

"Do you belong here? Do you want to belong here? Can you see
yourself being here next year? Or in years to come? What about the
other place?"

"What about it?"

"Do you belong *there*? Do you want to belong there? Can you see
yourself being there next year or in years to come? Can you let go of the
one and keep the other? Or do you have to keep both?"

"I'd rather lose the house than the apartment," he said.

"It means more to you?"

"It means something, but I don't know what that is. I'm just run-
ning back and forth."

"In your case, Lover Boy, the faster you run, the farther you have
to go until you know where you're going, yes, and until you let go of
your grievances."

"Then you decide, all of you. Tell me what to do."

"Wouldn't you rather leave me out of deciding for you, Lover Boy?"

He couldn't answer, feeling fallible, and he wouldn't say another word about it. Instead, he flopped down and lay on the blanket that was crumpled on the floor. Zouzou got up and said she was going off to help Priscilla with the laundry.

13

Cry, Cry, Cry

Came the moment when Lover Boy began a line of thinking that led to a kind of reckoning, alone in the dark. In the toiling of his mind, the line became a spiral, spiraling out of control. The trickster night came in the form of a judgement. He had to account for gains and losses, additions and subtractions of a working life. How had it come to this? He felt he couldn't move. He really couldn't think. Was this brain fog the result of the Covid he had once suffered, the Long Covid, as they were calling it? Was he delusional, or in a fugue state? He was inside his head, looking inward, taking the outside in, and had to get out of it. How could losers ever win? When losers win, winners have to lose. How could he resolve this apparent contradiction?

He uttered his pains as sounds of suffering when the body and mind are tired of all their wounds. He was carrying his sorrow in the shape of a man, a loser that cannot win. He suffered because he felt he suffered alone. But he wasn't alone. The women and the children were kneeling around him now, touching him in trying to comfort him. What was the true worth of this untouched pain, the worth of something when its ending grows into praise, instead of lamentation? A childhood friend of his, Bucky, (a nickname he carried as a result of his buckteeth and twisted, rabbity legs that made him walk/hop like a mechanical rabbit) used to say that *death must be comprehended in detail*. This in response to the death of his father. If death, then why not life? If life and death could be comprehended in detail, then how much more so must love? If love, what about work? And what about love and work together?

Now, in this place, in comprehending love and work in detail, Lover Boy surfaced from sadness and indecision, happy to know happiness as best it could be known, to know not what it *was*, but what happiness was *for*. They dealt with him as gently and tenderly as possible. What finally woke him was the sad cooing of a dove. The little girls couldn't wait to tell him that the bird had perched on the windowsill and had refused to fly away.

He saw Priscilla and Zouzou, and heard the children calling him, cooing about the dove, and also twittering with:

"Papa, papa. You were crying, while the dove was cooing."

"I couldn't help it," he said. "I'm sure the bird couldn't help it either. What if I cooed and the dove cried?"

Didn't the visitation of such a bird bring with it a message? What message? He cried until he laughed. The others laughed, until they almost cried.

"What are you doing, Lover Boy?" Zouzou wanted to know.

"Crying for myself and laughing at myself, too," he said.

They dried his eyes. Cry, cry, cry. Then moving in for a group-hug, lay on him as best they could. Even Bucco, recently returned from his outing, tried to swoop down on his body. They piled on. Then laughed and lifted him up to a standing position. The kids handed him his cane. He held them in an embrace as tightly as he could.

"The best is yet to come, Bucco said.

When he had prepared a spread for them, he plated it with a wonderful presentation of many culinary choices and options for all tastes. They helped themselves and each other. Zouzou told Lover Boy that it was *decided*: she wanted to be friends with Priscilla, and so, she and he would be good friends, too, without fringe benefits, despite the longing and need. This was her conception of a new arrangement, a new kind of family. He had to learn to love her beyond his desire for her perfect lips. No more hostility. No further humiliation. No more betrayal, or demoralization, just total cooperation. It had to be for everyone's sake, especially since Zouzou had fallen in love with the *babies*, as she called them, and wanted nothing to get in the way of loving them and being a part of their beautiful, little lives.

Bucco had news as well. Another decision had been made: he had contacted someone that Lover Boy knew, if not well, at least, in a poignant and immediate way, a man that had once hurt him and later had helped him to rescue Priscilla.

"Morphy?"

"Morphy," Bucco said. "You'll see him soon and hear what he has to offer. If you play your cards right, you can get to pay for both places, until you finally figure everything out. At least, you can keep them both for a while longer. Work, not hard, but smart, my friend, and don't comprise your vision of what is right and good for you and your family. After what you've been through, blame history. Blame the institutions. Blame the Virus. But never blame yourself. There's a great task for you to perform in all your tomorrows. Set your sights of that task: only you know what it is, and what it means. Look around here to get a better sense of what you have to do. Do it. Do it with purpose and meaning. Mean it all the time. Mean *everything*."

Was he secretly working for Dr. Sparrow? His talk certainly sounded like it. After eating the meal that he had prepared and served, Bucco drove Lover Boy to a meeting with Morphy. Lover Boy told Bucco that he wouldn't take part in any of Morphy's darker ventures, even if they only flirted with crime. Bucco said:

"He knows you can take it. He said he was impressed by your ability to endure and come out fighting without fighting back at all. He senses your capacity to get a job done, no matter the work."

When they got there, Lover Boy struggled up 4 flights to see Morphy. This time, he wasn't carrying bags. He was shown to a small office for his powwow with the man that had once punched him in the nose, the same man that had helped him get Priscilla back. The negotiations went back and forth with Morphy offering him work in all kinds of occupations from roofing to working on films and construction jobs and maintenance and delivery services.

"Jack-of-All-Trades."

"You can accept or walk away," Morphy said. "If you accept, I'll get you going and keep you going. That way, you can continue on your *rebellion*, and take care of your people."

"Why are you doing this?"

"Saw you in action. You can take a punch, carry a load, and you know how to keep your head down, keep your mouth shut, and move forward. Besides, you cleaned up after my dog. Something is owing to you."

Morphy was giving him work. Yes, or no? He had to decide. Morphy put his hand out for Lover Boy to shake and accept his offer. The worker slowly reached out his hand and shook on it. Yes? Or did it really mean No? Morphy had interests in a wide range of business opportunities from adult entertainment, say, to old gold dealer. Name it, he was involved in it.

"And I've got my pick?" Lover Boy asked.

"Pick," Morphy said. "I've got work for you for as long as you last. I warn you that I do *do* dark things, work of a darker and deadlier kind, but I'll keep you out of it, provided you keep working on the other interests in the kind of world you want to live in. Decide what works for you and just work your ass off, and live the way you want (or have) to live. Well?"

Lover Boy had to decide. Was he feeling his usual paralysis in the face of having to make a decision? What struck him about Morphy's offer of endless employment, job after job, with the promise of paycheck after paycheck, was the absurdity of his *paradoxical* position. He had wanted money to help overcome fear and insecurity regarding the possibility of failure. He had wanted to finance his so-called rebellion that sought the overthrow of a world he didn't like in favour of a way of living that made sense to him. Would the offer help him deal with fear/dread, or increase and intensify it/them? This was mockery of his intentions. The only response he could see at that moment was self-derision. Lover Boy felt like laughing at past actions, the carrying of bags, and the terror he experienced in the face of debt, pain, and impending collapse. His involvement with the Freedom Convoy was particularly laughable, even if the courts found the use of force "unreasonable." He had to mock it.

How could he stop from laughing? His laughter wasn't aimed at Morphy, or even at the nonsense of his own struggles, the farce that was his daily existence. Instead, he wanted to laugh at himself, especially at his fear, his feeling of emptiness and loss. The more he laughed, the more he sensed that he was no longer afraid. Fear wasn't to be avoided, but to be wished for.[6] He wanted his fear back again, not to confront or get rid of it, but to experience it in more depth, more panic, more horror in an ironic and rebellious state. That would strangely enough make it funnier.

When he and Bucco got back, he was just getting out of the truck when a guy he didn't know called out to him. He thought he wanted to fight, but he had something to say to Lover Boy, instead.

"Soon as I seen you," he said, "I couldn't help seeing that you look exactly like Elvis Presley from a certain period of the King's life. No kidding, man, the hair, the way your shirt is unbuttoned, but just a slightly different nose, as if Elvis had been in a brawl."

"You think I look like Elvis, despite the broken nose and the cane," Lover Boy said. "The only thing missing is the talent."

6   See Dr. Viktor Frankl's logotherapy.

"Don't you believe it," he said, "not for a minute. We've all got talent in our own way. I'm sure you do. Elvis lives. Thanks for letting me talk to you."

"Thanks for talking to me," Lover Boy said. "I do love Elvis."

14

Yes or No

Imagine, just while he was thinking of leaving the place, somebody came out of nowhere to affirm him with a kind of blessing or praise, even for his impersonation. Who knew it would happen there? Why was he so embarrassed about, and so ashamed of, the whole of his life?

Self-mockery of past fear and laughing at being compared to Elvis continued when he told Priscilla and Zouzou about Morphy's generous offer. Bucco already knew.

"Think about it," he said. "He's giving me a chance to work my ass off and to make money by the bagful, like garbage bags of dog poop that I once carried, loads of cash, working without end. The work, night and day, will help to overcome my fear about not having enough to finance my future scheme in life: to keep two places and two lives with two women and two kids."

Laughter was infectious. The others joined in with the self-professed *Fool*. They poked fun at themselves for the parts they had played in his comical schemes.

"The more I tried to face my fears, the more frightened I became," Lover Boy said. "The more I tried to overcome my anxiety about my indecisiveness, the more indecisive I was. Paralysis was the same. The more I tried to move, the more I couldn't move. I wanted everyone to hit me, punch me, punish me. But more and more hurt turned into continual and brutal punishment. The more I blamed myself for failure, the more I failed. If you worry about being good enough, you'll never be good enough."

"That's Lover Boy," Zouzou said.

"Lover Boy's back," Priscilla said.

"You should have been a comedian," Bucco said.

"I've been a Clown of the Freedom Convoy, a Fool of the Pandemic."

Over the days, weeks, months and years to come, for their amusement and his own, despite the embarrassment and shame, or because of them, he wouldd sometimes act out some of what he had gone through, like a mime ridiculing himself. Pretending to lift and carry bags would make him laugh at his stupidity and idiocy posing as courage and endurance. He would often perform the ride to Ottawa and the anarchic speeches he had made, including the absurd moment of his arrest. For that, he would lie face-down on the floor with arms behind his back, as if his wrists were being handcuffed. He would bang his forehead on the floor until somebody would plead for him to stop.

Lover Boy would stop hurting himself, but the laughter and derision would continue unabated. He would also act out the risible torture he had undergone at Shaydon's hands: a ridiculous boxer amateurishly boxing himself and losing every round, until finally the shadow knocked him out. He liked acting out some of the jobs he would have to do for Morphy. The family would applaud his pantomimes and depictions of endless toil and sacrifice. For what? The more money he made, the less he was able to keep, as always. Then he would deride his plans for the future and joke about his desperate attempt to pay his way out of sadness and despair.

In his performance that day, the jokes he told helped him to expose the lie of past motives and seemed to bring him back to his senses. They all laughed, enjoying Lover Boy's enjoyment.

"What are you going to say to Morphy?" Bucco had to know.

Would Lover Boy say, "No way, Morphy?" Would "Maybe" do to buy more time to think it over, and get a clearer picture of what he would be signing up for? He had searched for Morphy and had found him: a man that would kill you if you asked him to, or come to your aid in a rescue attempt, and a man who would kill you with work or kindness. Now, he wanted to take him on. Lover Boy could walk away, couldn't he? The word "Run" came to mind.

Was *striving* useless? Was failure beautiful, as some poets and philosophers suggested? It had been his search for Morphy that had unleashed the forces that opposed him, oppressed him, beat him down, and beat him up. He would have won had he wished not to win. That was the twist in the tale, the apparent contradiction that would help him to decide what to do and where to go. What would he have won, in an ironic sense, if he had played his cards right? Would he have been able to beat Morphy at his own game by not playing it? In winning, would he have become Morphy or Morphy-like? Yet Morphy had morphed from his enemy to his potential benefactor.

"How can he say *'Yes'*?" Priscilla said. "He'll kill himself with work, despite his new vision of what he wants to do with his life. We'll never see him, despite the easy money."

"How can he afford to say *'No'*?" Bucco jumped in. "He needs the money."

"If he says *'Yes,'* he'll live to regret it," Zouzou said. "If he says *'No,'* he may regret it at first, but in time, he'll make peace with it. Listen, we'll work together, not by scheming, but by living as a family. This is my family now, a new arrangement, a new way of living, that we'll all work for. No more feeling alone, or empty. No more loneliness and fear."

"I rented two places I could hardly afford," Lover Boy said, "but always felt homeless."

"What are you going to say to this Morphy, Lover Boy?"

Priscilla stood close to him, waiting for a reply. Was there a way of saying one thing, but meaning another? Was there a way of saying something, but meaning the opposite? Was this his technique or gambit of negating what was real and affirming what was not?

"I'm going to say the only thing I can say when I see him: that is, the only thing to say to guys like Morphy, and that is, the only way to keep laughing. Yes? No? Maybe?"

He was laughing at his own laughter. He poked fun at regretting, and all his regrets. He felt a sense, not of conclusion, but of emergence. Panic, loss and threat have come out the other side as gratitude and cooperation, and laughter.

"If I go, I'll regret it," he said. "If I stay, I'll likely regret it. Staying or going, I'll regret it. I would have won, if I hadn't lost, or not played at all. Who is going to let a loser win?"

"You would have won," Priscilla said, 'if you'd only played another game."

"The same for all games," he said, "when you play the way I do, even agreeing or disagreeing, deciding or not, is a losing game."

This was the comic fix that he, Jack (Lover Boy) Cade, as the laugher, was in. The trick was to mock himself even as he said "Yes," and to deprecate himself even on the point of saying "No." The laughing man was the butt of his own devious joke. The collector of grievances mocked his manner of collecting them. The comedian was not only the joker, but also the joke. He joked about the delirium-tainted dream visions and dreaming now that they were over. He even made a crack about calling his wife Priscilla when her real name was Marija.

"Now, Priscilla, or rather, my dear Marija, I'm walking with a limp," he said, for the sake of identification and identity.

"You're limping," she said, tearing up at the sound of her husband saying her real name, "but you've got to lead the way. We're with you."

Now, all that was left to do was laugh. The wile and stratagem to the kind of life he really *wanted* to live (and had to live) were sounded, not in the depths of a ceaseless exclamation of *money*, but rather in a new battle cry: *love and work,* kept together by *laughter*. What was clear or clearer was that he saw it clearly now, as clearly as the others saw it. Sometimes, the telling of his workman's tale or fable felt like filling in time sheets or reports, or applying for jobs he could never get, or were denied him. Now, his tale was like a joke that needed a punchline about a loser. Moving forward, no matter how dark or bitter they were, often to the amusement of Ana and Lina and the others, while performing his stand-up routines about his worker's fable, laughing and loving, the ironic punchline of his best or worst joke about that weird period of his life, feeling the dis-ease of the universal disease, was:

"I would have won, if only I had refused to play."[7]

That time, Ana and Lina cheered, performing a tiny, perfect victory dance.

"You won, Papa. You won."

"Thanks," he said, laughing, taking their little hands in his. "The loser won."

"You're getting the last laugh," Bucco said.

"Am I? Or is it the first"

"A laugh is a laugh," he said.

Now they laughed and doubled as dancers: from 3 to 6. Priscilla, Zouzou and Bucco joined in, moving clockwise and then counterclockwise, widening the winner's circle, especially when the dog joined in.

"Who won?" they chanted, spinning round and round.

"He won," Zouzou said, seeing his one-and-only moral victory as that of a soon-to-be-defeated prizefighter winning in the last round.

"Papa won," Ana and Lina said, innocent of the game.

"Lover Boy won," Priscilla (Mariya) said, reading the moral as if of a worker's fable. "Say it, Lover Boy, say, '*I won*.'"

7   "You win if you don't want to play." (*Jokers Wild*, Nic Labriola)

What could he possibly say, dancing with his daughters as he was, and capering with the others? The women and the girls seemed to be taking up his cause. What was it? What should he say to those that loved him? Was it a sad win, if it was a win, or a happy loss, if that was what it really was? Since his wife said so, echoing the other voices, and since Ana and Lina were spinning around him, like tiny, perfect dervishes, lightly and brightly caught between the quickness of laughter and the vestiges of fear, Lover Boy said *it* for the sake of the fun-loving dancers and the funny victory dance. Was this how a worker's fable was supposed to end? The whole story was in his life and not his version of it.

"I won, and this is what happens when losers win," Lover Boy said, as comically lightly, and as self-mockingly brightly, as he could, and no longer *beggin'* for money, work, love or even mercy, and no need of his *beggin'* letter, because this was where his tale about an unlikely winner was really supposed to begin.

Notes

Frankl, Viktor E. (Viktor Emil), 1905-1997 author. *Man's Search for Meaning: An Introduction to Logotherapy*. Boston: Beacon Press, 1962.

My gratitude goes to my son, Nic Labriola, for his example, and for borrowings from his one-act play, *Joker's Wild* and other texts.

The name, Jack Cade, is derived from the rebel in Shakespeare's *Henry VI Part 2*. Cade's rebellious speeches depend on social grievances and anti-authoritarian feelings to support his rebellion.

The Covid-19 Pandemic (or the coronavirus pandemic) began in 2019. It was a global outbreak that caused serious health problems, as well as social and political disruptions and clashes.

The Freedom Convoy protest in Canada began on January 29, 2022 when convoys descended on Ottawa with a convergence on Parliament Hill. Thousands of protesters joined the movement. Prime Minister Trudeau used the Emergencies Act to dismantle the protest in an attempt to restore order, though protests against him and his government persisted long after the event.

www.ingramcontent.com/pod-product-compliance
Lightning Source LLC
Chambersburg PA
CBHW020729250626
47155CB00006B/2223